Exploring Dark Short Fiction #7: A Primer to Gemma Files

Exploring Dark Short Fiction (A Primer Series) Created by Eric J. Guignard

#1: A Primer to Steve Rasnic Tem (Dark Moon Books, 2017)

#2: A Primer to Kaaron Warren (Dark Moon Books, 2018)

#3: A Primer to Nisi Shawl (Dark Moon Books, 2018)

#4: A Primer to Jeffrey Ford (Dark Moon Books, 2019)

#5: A Primer to Han Song (Dark Moon Books, 2020)

#6: A Primer to Ramsey Campbell (Dark Moon Books, 2021)

#7: A Primer to Gemma Files (Dark Moon Books, 2024)

Fiction Written by Eric J. Guignard

Doorways to the Deadeye (JournalStone, 2019)

A Graveside Gallery: Tales of Ghosts and Dark Matters (Cemetery Dance Publications, 2025)

Last Case at a Baggage Auction (Harper Day Books, 2020)

That Which Grows Wild: 16 Tales of Dark Fiction (Cemetery Dance Publications, 2018)

Anthologies Edited by Eric J. Guignard

After Death... (Dark Moon Books, 2013)

Dark Tales of Lost Civilizations (Dark Moon Books, 2012)

Fantasmagoriana Deluxe (with Leslie S. Klinger) (Dark Moon Books, 2023)

The Five Senses of Horror (Dark Moon Books, 2018)

+Horror Library+ Volume 6 (Cutting Block Books/ Dark Moon Books, 2017)

+Horror Library+ Volume 7 (Dark Moon Books, 2022)

+Horror Library+ Volume 8 (Dark Moon Books, 2023)

Pop the Clutch: Thrilling Tales of Rockabilly, Monsters, and Hot Rod Horror (Dark Moon Books, 2019)

Professor Charlatan Bardot's Travel Anthology to the Most (Fictional) Haunted Buildings in the Weird, Wild World (Dark Moon Books, 2021)

Scaring and Daring (HarperCollins, 2025)

A World of Horror (Dark Moon Books, 2018)

**The Horror Writers Association Presents: Haunted Library of Horror Classics
Edited by Eric J. Guignard and Leslie S. Klinger**

Vol. I: The Phantom of the Opera by Gaston Leroux (Sourcebooks, 2020)

Vol. II: The Beetle by Richard Marsh (Sourcebooks, 2020)

Vol. III: Vathek by William Beckford (Sourcebooks, 2020)

Vol. IV: The House on the Borderland by William Hope Hodgson (Sourcebooks, 2020)

Vol. V: Of One Blood: or, The Hidden Self by Pauline Hopkins (Sourcebooks, 2021)

Vol. VI: The Parasite and Other Tales of Terror by Arthur Conan Doyle (Sourcebooks, 2021)

Vol. VII: The King in Yellow by Robert W. Chambers (Sourcebooks, 2021)

Vol. VIII: Ghost Stories of an Antiquary by M.R. James (Sourcebooks, 2021)

Vol. IX: Gothic Classics: The Castle of Otranto by Horace Walpole (Sourcebooks, 2022)

Vol. X: The Mummy! by Jane Webb (Sourcebooks, 2022)

Exploring Dark Short Fiction #7: A Primer to Gemma Files

Edited by Eric J. Guignard
Commentary by Michael Arnzen, PhD
Illustrations by Michelle Prebich

DARK MOON BOOKS
Los Angeles, California

EXPLORING DARK SHORT FICTION #7: A PRIMER TO GEMMA FILES
Copyright © Eric J. Guignard 2025

Edited by Eric J. Guignard
Interior layout by Eric J. Guignard
Cover design by Eric J. Guignard
www.ericjguignard.com

Commentary by Michael Arnzen, PhD
www.gorelets.com

Interior illustrations by Michelle Prebich
www.batinyourbelfry.etsy.com

"In the Poor Girl Taken by Surprise" © 2004 by Gemma Files. First published in *The Worm in Every Heart*, Prime Books/ Wildside Press.
"Slick Black Bones and Soft Black Stars" © 2012 by Gemma Files. First published in *A Season in Carcosa*, edited by Joseph S. Pulver, Sr., Miskatonic River Press.
"Venio" © 2019 by Gemma Files. First published in *Vastarien*, vol. 2, #1, Spring, Grimscribe Press.
"Sown from Salt" © 2008 by Gemma Files. First published in *The Harrow*, vol. 11, #12, December, www.theharrow.com.
"Guising" © 2015 by Gemma Files. First published in *October Dreams II: A Celebration of Halloween*, edited by Richard Chizmar and Robert Morrish, Cemetery Dance Publications.
"Found Footage Storytelling, or Writing Epistolary Narratives for the 21st Century" © 2021 by Gemma Files. First published in *Writers Workshop of Horror 2*, edited by Michael Knost, Hydra Publications.

First edition published in February, 2025

Library of Congress Cataloging-in-Publication Data
Exploring dark short fiction #7: a primer to Gemma Files) / Eric J. Guignard.

Library of Congress Control Number: 2021940391
ISBN-13: 978-1-949491-47-0 (hardback)
ISBN-13: 978-1-949491-45-6 (trade paperback)
ISBN-13: 978-1-949491-46-3 (e-book)

DARK MOON BOOKS
Los Angeles, California
www.DarkMoonBooks.com
Made in the United States of America

(V102924)

This book is dedicated to those who encourage the written word, those who seek a deeper understanding of literature, and those who simply love dark fiction.

And of course, this is dedicated also to Gemma Files, an inspiration to so many. Thank you for consenting to this project.

TABLE OF CONTENTS

INTRODUCTION
BY ERIC J. GUIGNARD

GEMMA FILES ISN'T ONE TO WORRY MUCH ABOUT labels. She writes fantasy. She writes weird. She writes erotica, horror, alternate history. She writes progressive, pervasive, genre-busting tales of terror and tragedy and love and redemption. She writes what she wants. So, label? Perhaps "Revered Writer of the Fantastic" might suit. Of course, besides authoring fiction, she's also been a journalist, film critic, poet, teacher, screenwriter, and more. There's little Gemma hasn't been involved in within the enclaves of academia and creative output since first publishing in the early 1990s. Truly, finding the right label to place on her that's so broad and all-encompassing to capture everything Gemma is and does is a daunting (perhaps inconceivable) task. But it doesn't stop people from trying.

Publishers Weekly says Gemma is an author of "unflinching prose sprinkled with touches of gore." *National Public Radio* describes her as "A voice that is colorful, powerful, and charismatic." *Locus Magazine* says she is the author for "horror aficionados who delight in dread." Albeit, though each of those is true and accurate, for my own purpose I'm going to stick with "Revered Writer of the Fantastic." And I go back to that simply because it's what she means to *me*.

I don't know of any other author (except perhaps the late,

great Tanith Lee) who can write so broadly, so prolifically, and so *darkly* a fiction tale. And when I say "darkly," I mean there is no taboo Gemma Files will not touch (which I declare with the highest of praise and as one who generally avoids literature that oversteps boundaries of inappropriateness). To wit, the first time I read Gemma was her stunning short story "The Emperor's Old Bones" (in Ellen Datlow and Terri Windling's *The Year's Best Fantasy & Horror: Thirteenth Annual Collection*), which involves a litany of some of the most traumatic topics imaginable (including "off-screen" cannibalism of children). But content such as this is not written by Gemma for shock, but rather as means to an end; it's utter horror that buttresses a harrowing, beautifully told story of twisted love, magic, survival, and hope in an epic adventure of escape from World War II-torn China and the consequences arising from the simple desperation for survival. Still, decades later, that story remains with me; it haunts me, as much the story itself as the author's razor-perceptive voice.

And since then, every story I've read by Gemma Files has been a correlative experience, memorable and vicious and startling, most often going in unexpected directions. It's a hallmark of Gemma Files that a tale may start out shimmering in nascent eclipse and then reverse itself, turning to full dark, or perhaps full light, for not all her stories are those of tragedy and gloom, but also of atonement, glamor, and defiance to social constraint. Gemma imbues her cross-genre work with layers like dark stratum: heartbreak upon horror, built over the vignettes of life we may find ourselves in, but for that one slight turn of reality. Take, for example, the after-life mysticism of necrophiliac sex shows in "Kissing Carrion;" or a reimagined poetic and tormented Jack the Ripper in "Jack-Knife;" recognition that loneliness is just as melancholic for dark spirits as it is for the adolescent-living in "Hell Friend;" or the gallows-humor-rich recompense of a desperate thief meeting his victim's governess in "Nanny Grey." And such are stories I chose *not* to include in this Primer, for what *does* await may well provide—if not a label—at least a more penetrating survey of the author's far-reaching inventiveness and panache, with explorations of inverted lore, biblical weird western, Lovecraftian mythos, and more.

Named "One of the genre's most original and innovative voices" (*L.A. Review of Books*) and "An expert at terrifying prose" (*LitReactor*), Gemma Files has been penning gritty and macabre fiction for over three decades, earning multiple industry awards (International Horror Guild Award, Shirley Jackson Award, Sunburst Award, Bram Stoker Award (twice), etc.) and critical acclaim from pundits, fans, and peers alike.

Following is this humble introduction to her work, seventh in a continuing series intended to celebrate modern masters of literary short fiction. And I hope upon its conclusion, dear reader, you will agree with my own empathic label: "Revered Writer of the Fantastic."

Midnight cheers,

—Eric J. Guignard
Chino Hills, California
July 21, 2024

ABOUT GEMMA FILES

AN AUTOBIOGRAPHICAL ACCOUNT

THE BASICS: I WAS BORN ON APRIL 4, 1968, IN London, England, within the sound of Bow Bells (which supposedly makes a Cockney, though please don't tell any real Cockneys that, because they'll laugh like hell). My parents were both actors, both trained at the National Theatre School in Montreal, Quebec; my Dad (Gary Files), previously a graphic artist, decided to emigrate to Canada from Australia in order to avoid being sent to Vietnam for the war, while my mother (Elva Mai Hoover) first applied at age fifteen but was too young to be accepted, so she stuck around in Montreal working various jobs under the counter until she turned sixteen. He graduated first and went to England, where she later joined him, they married, et cetera. I came out simultaneously premature but overdeveloped, my skin grey—this was the era when doctors told pregnant women to keep, or possibly take up smoking, so they wouldn't gain too much weight—and dry, with a full head of hair and long fingernails. In another age, people might have thought I was doomed to become a werewolf.

My parents went back to Canada—settling in downtown Toronto, Ontario—when I was roughly a year and a half old. Eventually, they discovered they weren't suited to live the rest of their lives in each other's company, for reasons I didn't really understand until much later. My father moved out when I was eight or so, the year they sat me down and told me that Dad was going to go live somewhere else. "Don't ever think it's your fault," he told me on his way out, thus assuring that I *would* think it was my fault, for roughly the rest of my young adulthood. Of course, him moving back to Australia within a few more years probably didn't help with that.

I remember it felt a bit like that time when I'd accidentally run out in front of a car while playing cops and robbers in the lane out back of our previous house—the impact wasn't something I remembered directly, just its aftermath. Just suddenly realizing I must have bounced off the bumper and gone down straight between the front two wheels with my arms and legs magically folded *the exact right way* to avoid getting run over, because I was now lying beneath the car looking up at its underside with oil dripping onto my scraped leg and urine pooling through my skirt, matting it to the dust: wet, warm, cold, stunned. My head hurt. I was too surprised to cry. It took four neighborhood guys, including my dad, to tip the car far enough off of me for Mom and a few other neighborhood women to drag me out. And then it was over.

Now extend that extremely upsetting experience further; stretch it over years. A sort of decade-long concussion, an absolute rupture of established routine, during which I found it hard to make friends or keep them, to understand why I was apparently "too much" for everyone around me, including my own family: too angry, too odd, too selfish, too eccentric, too smart, too stupid. Always moving, always forgetting the rules, always bullied, always a bully. And no one to lift the car off me, either.

Glasses, braces, puberty at ten and a half. I was tall enough to get into Restricted films by eleven, but I still couldn't understand how to have a conversation that didn't involve me monologuing about stuff no one else was interested in. And eventually, on some level, I think I figured out that the best way to avoid getting permanently stuck in a series of memory loops during which I constantly relived yet another moment of embarrassment, rage, and self-hatred was to simply absent myself—to learn to daydream, to walk down the street with my nose in a book, to almost physically inhabit the movies I watched, to flush my old memory banks as fully as possible, then refuse to form any new memories at all.

That last part's impossible, obviously—but I did try. Which is why I often find I have to think fairly hard in order to remember my past in detail, and even then, it's always a question of whether I want to see what happened without being able to feel it, or feel what happened without being able to see it. Things come to me at one remove, as if glimpsed through a thick, well-scratched porthole, the helmet of a diving bell I'm trapped inside, woozy with incipient bends. I go down and down through darkness, peering about me, trying to recognize things: Is that me? Are those my parents? Canada or Australia? Before or after? At a certain point, I taught myself to separate emotionally from my own experiences, to stop myself from having to relive things while I remembered them. I never seemed to have strong memories of pleasure, only of painful moments of self-reflection, weird little scars built around sudden realizations of having let myself or those around me down, the guilt of being me.

Bad jokes. Not being able to express myself clearly. Being treated like a child. Being betrayed by my own instincts. Not understanding what was really going on. Being mocked for not understanding. That time I shit myself in the pool. That time I forgot my gloves at the skating rink and watched my hands turn dead white, then wept with pain as they defrosted. That time I knocked my front teeth out sliding face-first down a hill. That time someone threw a snowball with rock inside it at me for walking by them, broke my glasses, and almost scratched my cornea. That time I fell asleep before a friend was supposed to come over, woke to find her already here, then cried for half an hour because I "missed" her arrival. That time I had stomach flu, couldn't keep myself from puking all over my own bed, then immediately puked again at the smell of my own vomit.

That's how my own feelings felt, to me: Like a punch in the gut, a disgusting upheaval. For years, my first reaction whenever something I read, watched, or listened to "made" me cry was to think: *Oh, fuck YOU. Don't stick your hand inside my chest and wiggle it around and tell me it's great to be sensitive; don't piss in my ear and tell me it's raining.*

So yeah, it became necessary to separate my feelings from my memories, to observe them through a scrim of pure objectivity, even to discard them entirely if possible, ostensibly in order to make room for other stuff—the Sherlock Holmes method. There are sections of my life I remember very little from, therefore; I have proof they happened, I guess, but they can't hurt me anymore.

Not unless I let them.

The primary-to-middle school system chewed me up and spat me out, but my mom discovered there were these things called alternative schools, and that helped (along with six or so years of therapy)—I went to one, then another. I graduated with grades good enough to get me into university. I paid half my own way through journalism school, working crap jobs instead of internships that could have helped me when I graduated into a recession.

It was 1990; I worked as a floor attendant at a high-end sex shop until I couldn't take talking to customers anymore (imposter syndrome is a scourge, probably even when you aren't a lifelong introvert who suffers from resting bitch-face), then worked night-shift security and wrote terrible screenplays in between patrolling various empty buildings. I sold articles here and there as a stringer for *eye Weekly*, a Toronto arts and culture magazine, then eventually switched to a more permanent position reviewing films for them, which allowed me to move into my first apartment.

I continued to work for *eye* for roughly nine years, during which I eventually began first placing short stories with various independent horror venues, then teaching at two different diploma mills offering film production courses. In 1998, I sold five short stories to *The Hunger*, an erotic horror anthology show produced by Tony and Ridley Scott's Scott Free Productions company for the cable TV network Showtime, and used that experience to expand my various classes on film history, Canadian film history, screenwriting, and TV series development. In 1999, meanwhile, my story "The Emperor's Old Bones" won the International Horror Guild Award for Best Short Fiction. I went to Denver to accept my tiny gargoyle, where I was surprised to discover that people I'd been reading since I was a teenager actually knew who I was. While there, I cut a deal for my first two collections of short fiction, *Kissing Carrion* and *The Worm in Every Heart*.

I kept writing when I wasn't teaching or reviewing, my "short" work getting steadily longer and longer, yet never quite becoming novel-length. I married (to Stephen J. Barringer, my "each thing I show you is a piece of my death" co-author). We had a son (his name is Callum).

Things really began to change, however, when life dealt me

what seemed at the time like yet another triple sucker-punch: I lost my job at *eye* (frozen out after they switched editors, for being far too old to work at their hot, hip young mag anymore), then lost my job teaching after switching to it full-time when the school I now worked at was shut down by its parent company, right around the same time that my son was diagnosed with Autism Spectrum Disorder. I sunk into a slough of despond, failing to make the jump from short fiction to novels by the time I turned forty, which naturally meant I was worthless; I spent the next year writing nothing but *3:10 to Yuma* fanfiction (remake, not classic) and feeling sorry for myself, while also learning everything about being an autism mom.

The good part, in retrospect, was that I began to move toward the realization that genetics would tend to suggest I might well be on the spectrum somewhere myself—that if people had been looking for Asperger's Syndrome in girls back when I was at my absolute worst (or Asperger's at all, really), then I might have avoided spending most of my life thus far feeling like there was something inherently, unfixably "wrong" with me... but much like Cal's diagnosis, I wouldn't entirely accept that idea for a few years yet.

The far *better* part, however, is that the year I turned forty-one, I looked at the 100,000 words' worth of fanfic I'd written about Charlie Prince and Ben Wade gettin' it on and thought: *Well shit, I guess I* can *write something novel-length, after all. How about forgetting about salability, and just doing what turns you on (literally)?* By April, my friends Brett Savory and Sandra Kasturi had decided to start their own publishing imprint, ChiZine Publications (named after *The Chiaroscuro* webzine, Brett's previous project), and began asking every writer they knew if they were working on a book. "By coincidence, yes," was my reply.

CZP published my first novel, *A Book of Tongues*, which soon became a trilogy known as the Hexslinger series (*AboT, A Rope of Thorns, A Tree of Bones*)—Weird Western shoot-'em-up action with black magic and reborn Mexica gods plus a big gay romance in the middle, oh my. I followed that up with a story-cycle in the Alice Munro urban fantasy mode called *We Will All Go Down Together: Stories of the Five-Family Coven* and, eventually, my first standalone horror novel: *Experimental Film,* in which I plundered my own life experiences to fashion the tale of a potentially neurodiverse former film critic-turned-film teacher with an autistic son who discovers both a lost Canadian silent era movie-maker and the not-so-dead goddess that woman just may have captured on film. The book went on to win a Shirley Jackson Award for Best Novel and a Sunburst Award for Best Adult Novel, moving me to the level of my career I occupy today.

Let's be real: None of that would have happened without Brett, Sandra, and CZP, which is what makes what happened next so incredibly sad. After working themselves into the ground creating a diverse and vivid Canadian dark fiction scene centered around Ontario, two of the best friends I've ever had watched the same company they'd both given so much of themselves to collapse over roughly a month, brought down by a storm of tweets, Facebook posts, and online articles. Having given at least one quote I really wish I hadn't at the time, I'm not going to comment any further on the situation except to say that you're entirely free to Google it yourselves if you're interested, and draw your own conclusions.

What I will say, however, is that I now consider November

of 2019 to be the single most painful moment of my professional life to this point. I lost friends, but I'm okay; I got my intellectual property back, signed with Open Road Media to make sure my books stayed in print, went on to win a Bram Stoker Award for my most recent collection. My friends? They lost *everything*.

And there you have it. I'm almost fifty-five now, still married, and my son is a young adult; we've spent the last few years going through the same stuff as everybody else, but things are nevertheless better than they've ever been. I'm a preliminary sketch of a crone (though not, my husband vociferously assures me, visually), an elder and a mentor, a firm proponent of monster pride. Still orbiting the rim of the same black hole as everybody else, still uncertain what will happen when I finally get sucked down inside of it, the way we all eventually will. Still aware that love comes with pain inside it, and that the main problem with being human is knowing everything ends.

Still writing horror, and happy to keep on doing so, forever.

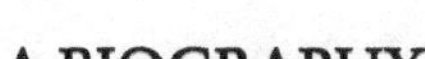

A BIOGRAPHY

BORN IN LONDON, ENGLAND AND RAISED IN Toronto, Canada, Gemma Files has been an award-winning horror author since 1999 (when her story "The Emperor's Old Bones" won the International Horror Guild Award for Best Short Fiction). She has published five novels (including the 2015 Shirley Jackson Award-winning *Experimental Film*, from CZP), six collections of short fiction (including the 2021 Bram Stoker Award-winning *In That Endlessness, Our End*, from Grimscribe Press), and four collections of speculative poetry. Her most recent works are *Dark Is Better* (Trepidatio) and *Blood From The Air* (Grimscribe).

In the Poor Girl Taken by Surprise

THIS IS AN OLD STORY. MOST STORIES ARE. ANYONE who says different is lying, or perhaps simply misinformed.

But thus, and even so:

Once upon a time, my darlings, these woods were full of wolves—yes, even here in the wilds of Upper Canada, where the light which seeps between evergreens and maple trees alike is as brown and stinging as though it comes filtered through a thousand mosquito wings at once. Here where the sky is clogged with bark and cobwebs, where black biting flies hover thick under the branches and each step stirs the pine-needle loam up like hay, or sodden grey-brown snow; here amongst the tangle of crab-apple trees and blackthorn bushes, where even the quietest footfall is enough to send little toads hopping clear, like brown clumps of dirt with tiny, jewelled eyes . . .

Even here in these dim and man-empty places, where things leap from tree to tree far overhead, just out of sight. Where under the mulch and muck of dead leaves a veritable feast of dust lies waiting—a fine, dun carpet of ground and yellowed bones.

Which is why, if you hear footsteps behind you as you make your way along the forest's paths, it may be best to stop and hide and wait—as quietly as possible—until they pass you by. And if you see something high in the leaves above, something that looks like eyes travelling fast through the darkness, it may be best to ignore it, even if one is sure it can only be swamp gas—though in truth, there are few real swamps nearby, unless that sump of downed maples and frozen mud you struggled your way through to get to The Poor Girl Taken By Surprise tonight counts as such.

For there are so many things in these woods left still uncounted, even now: Trees whose branches rise high as church-spires, a perfect shape for the keels of bewitched canoes to scrape themselves upon. Caves in which squat the dried-out corpses of savages, hunted beyond endurance and sick with strange diseases, who starved to death rather than allow themselves to be captured and corralled like animals; their hungry ghosts may yet be heard keening at twilight, ill-wishing any White man whose shadow dares to cross their doorstep. A lake that goes up and a cathedral that goes down and a woman dressed all in birch-bark walking, rustling, with her left hand clutched tightly to her chest—that dead-white skeleton hand whose touch to the unwary forehead means madness, whose touch to the unwary back means death . . .

Yet here we sit snug and warm and dry nonetheless, traders and settlers and immigrants bound for even more distant places alike, before this open, welcoming fire; here we may eat and drink our fill and go 'round the circle in turn, each of we travelers swapping a story for our place beneath this roof 'till morning. And I will be more than glad to add my own contribution to that roster, if only it should please you to bend your ear and listen.

Might it be that you have a place already set at your table for a poor old woman such as I, *Monsieur*? *Madame*? A place at your sideboard for a starving, childless widow, *mesdames et messieurs, s'il vous plait?*

Oh, no matter; I have walked far tonight, expecting to go yet farther, before I saw your sign and heard your merriment. But I am not yet so weak with hunger that I cannot seat myself.

Once upon a time, and a time it was . . .

. . . there were two sisters who lived all alone, with no mother and no father to care for them, in the very deepest and darkest part of the woods. They lived in the house of their grandmother, who was often away on long trips, but they were not lonely, these two; never so, not in each other's company. For they were used, from long experience, to making their own amusements.

And what brought this lopsided little family to the heart of the forest, *deux gamines* and one old woman, so far away from everything that is soft, feminine, and civilized? Their property dated back to before the Plains of Abraham, before the French Revolution; granted land in perpetuity, as dowry and domain, 'till one of them might be inclined to sell or give it away—and if that sounds like a curse rather than a gift, then so be it. A not-so-self-imposed exile in the no longer-New World for reasons untold, or (at least) unspoken.

The name, *messieurs*? Ah, but our names have come to mean so very little here in this empty country of ours, have they not? Just as our definitions tend to . . . shift, down the centuries. *Tessedaluye, Tesse-dal'oeuil, Tête-de-l'oueil*—"head of the eye," no? Or perhaps a misapprehension never corrected: Head of something very, very different. *L'oueil, la luce, la loup* . . .

And so it was, after all: *Tête-du-loup*, "head of the wolf." Wolf's-head.

A strange name, certainly. And yet I know it as well as though it were—my own.

The savages who had occupied this particular plot of land began to shun it soon after the family first arrived to take possession of their new hunting-grounds. For they were ferocious hunters, these ones, male and female alike; from winter through spring, summer and fall, each season to its own sort of prey. In the old country, it had been whispered that the Tessedaluye kept their own calendar, and maybe even their own prayer-book too—had pledged themselves neither wholly to the Catholic nor the Huguenot faith, in those dark days after Catherine de' Medici and her brood split France limb from limb, twisting the wound so that it would never heal cleanly again. Which made them no sort of Christians at all, perhaps.

Or not *good* ones, at any rate.

And where was this house, you ask? Oh, not so very far from here at all. Not so *very* far that they were not often diverted by the light and noise of The Poor Girl Taken By Surprise, which spilled toward them from across the lake, since they had never seen a public-house before, or travelers in such numbers: Music, laughter, the rumble of ox-carts, bright city-bought fabrics, men and women dancing like leaves in the wind. These things were mysteries and amazements to the two sisters, poor solitary bumpkins that they were!

For they knew many things, these girls, you see, though the ways of Man were not among them. How to trap a rabbit and skin it. How to tell the track of stag from that of moose. How to cook a hedgehog under an earthenware bowl, peel its stinging quills free, and crack it for its tender meat. What parts of every creature may be dried for carrying, which must be hung awhile before they become palatable, which may be pickled, or otherwise preserved. And which parts are best eaten just as they are, raw and red and dripping, on the very spot where they were butchered.

The human animal, only, was one they had never hunted. Let alone...

...tasted.

Girls are curious creatures, a fact their grandmother was well acquainted with—fated to be wild in their season, just as she had been in hers. So even though she understood that her warnings would (in all probability) go unheeded, she was constrained to voice them anyway.

Come close, my darlings, come closer; listen to me a while, before I go where I must. We do not meddle with those we do not know, yes? Therefore keep always to the safest path, the well-trod road of needles rather than the easier-seeming road of pins—back and forth to Grandmother's house, where you may pull the bobbin, and the latch will go up, open the door and come in.

And perhaps you should have stayed behind, old woman, if you feared so for their safety; this is what you may be thinking, and not without cause. But we cannot always choose the way things happen. I have my habits and my instincts, just as they . . . did.

A cry from the back, now: You, sir, *repetez-vous*? Ah, *were they pretty*, of course. For the most important questions much be answered first, naturally.

Well. We all know the tale of Rose Red and Snow White, do we not? From which one may gather that one was coarse and the other fine, one dark and the other fair. One might have been considered pretty, even in this company. The other—

—the other, not so much.

It was winter by then, which made things harder. Winter settles hard upon us all in this inhospitable place, am I mistaken? For when the light grows thin and the nights long, there is very little to amuse one's self with, aside from sleep. Or hunting, when the hunger takes you, which is often enough.

The people at the inn, also hungry—some of you here amongst them, no doubt—tried their hand at hunting as well. But when one does not know the territory, *c'est difficile*. The girls watched their distress mount, counting down the days to their grandmother's return, and I think that it must have seemed to them that without their aid, the men and women of The Poor Girl Taken By Surprise must surely pine and die like bear-cubs woken too early, beaver kits trapped in an icebound lodge . . . for they were tender-hearted creatures, as all girls are. Yes, indeed.

Almost as much so as they were also born hunters, long-used to watching and waiting while prey struggled deeper and deeper into its own trap. To check for signs of struggle in the snow or drops of blood in the underbrush, for the uneven prints of some weakened thing, for whatever Nature herself might have selected—pre-ordained, in her own magnanimous way—for them to cull.

The Feast of Stephen, Saint Stephen's Day, has long been set aside for charity. So that was the day our two sisters set out for the inn across the lake, bearing gifts with which to barter their welcome: Furs they had cured themselves, berries and fruits they had stored, a goodly portion of meat left over from their own store-room.

How they must have smiled when they drew within sight of these doors, as the moon rose and the snow began to fall—a night much like this one, come to think! For inside was light, warmth, and singing, peddlers with their wares spread out on tables, all manner of strange and interesting folk from all manner of places they had never dreamed on, let alone been. And how the inn's inhabitants must have smiled to see them coming, also: These two girls, unaccompanied, with their basket of goods and their gawky, gawping stares. Like veritable manna from Heaven.

I was far away by then, *mes amis*, following my quarry under a lead-colored snow-storm sky. Yet I do believe, nevertheless, that I can reckon the very moment during which my granddaughters' rash actions led them somewhere they had never wanted to be.

You at the back—yes, you: I have no doubt you thought my Sylvie "pretty," when you knew her. And my Perrinette, with her puppyish ways; you must have thought her a bad bargain in comparison, though well worth the price of such company. When you fed them both grog and gin, played your fiddles and dared them to dance with each other, dressed them up in your cheap whores' cast-offs and rouged their lips and cheeks to make them look more . . . appetizing? *Oui, madame, c'est véritable*: I know for a fact that you were there that night as chief inciter, if not ring-leader, in those drunken revels. And how, you may well ask?

Let us say that if I wrinkle my nose just so, I can—without a doubt—

—smell it on you.

Their only mistake—the "sin" that condemned them—was that they had never learned how men, too, prey on men, poor little ones. I had spared them that knowledge, foolishly, out of some vain hope of preserving their innocence; far too well, as it turns out. And for that I will no doubt have to make amends, in time.

This glittering mess-hall, this carbuncle, squatting over a field of shallow graves. This poisoned honeycomb, a nest to trap and drown flies in. This place where off-season travelers sometimes simply disappear, leaving nothing but their few sad treasures, and a table or so of full bellies, behind.

But you were surprised as well, I am sure, when—after the girls saw you, for the first time, in your true shapes—they let you see them, in *theirs*.

My Sylvie found a thin place in the ice with her paw as they broke from the inn, and sank like a stone to its bottom. But my poor Perrinette, hampered by her fine new clothing, was easily brought to ground. And though she snapped at you with her slavering jaws and tore at you with her clever, clawed hands, you shot her all the same: Put a ball in her brain, tore her limb from limb, flayed her wolf's skin away from the man-skin still lurking below, then dragged what was left of her back inside.

For there is much meat to be had from a wolf, if one knows where to make the cuts. Almost as much, in the end, as there is on a poor girl, taken by surprise.

—⁂—

Yes, it is a sad story indeed. And though you do not seem eager to hear the end of it, I will tell it to you, all the same.

These woods were full of wolves when we first came, but we drove them out, hunting them almost to their extinction. For they knew the truth of our nature, just as the savages did: We are the sort who do not care to share what is ours, not even with our closest kin. So when the wolves had fled we hunted savages instead, and because we hunted them, the savages dressed up like us and prayed to us, prayed to us not to eat them. We became their gods for a time, until they fled as well, to find themselves others. Or—perhaps—to seek out a place with none.

But we are not gods, and never have been. We are Wolf's-heads. *Tessedaluye.* We are . . .

. . . shall I really have to say the word aloud, my friends?

The primal sin of those like myself, *mes amis*, is that because we were once people who acted like beasts, we are forever cursed to be beasts who know they were once men. A wolf hunts in a pack, to eat, not to kill—it is a proponent of all those most wonderful, natural qualities: Liberty, loyalty, fraternity. But a were-wolf hunts to kill rather than eat, a creature whose unslaked hunger is only for blood and slaughter, defilement and degradation. It will prey even on its own family, for the bonds of kinship mean startlingly little to it; it can violate the families of others, and will, for much the same reason. The were-wolf likes to play, to torture, and takes a grim humor in its continual masquerade, the toothy animal face beneath the gentle human mask.

Perhaps this is because the oldest story behind the myth—one which those amongst us educated in the Classics may well recognize—is that of King Lykaon and his fifty sons; Lykaon, whose disgusting crimes caused the old god Zeus to flood the known world, washing it clean for future, less perverse occupants. Lykaon and his sons, who were transformed into wolves for profaning and denying the gods, for serving strangers human meat, for ravening the land they were supposed to protect like bandits rather than rulers. And since sometimes Lykaon's name is linked with that of Tantalus, perhaps it follows that the rule he broke was the one which warns us not to share in the eating of our own children, or others'. For to force or trick others into sharing the flesh of your own line is always an evil sort of victory over them, a potential spreading of moral contagion.

Later, in Arcadia, followers of the cult of Lykaian Zeus believed that each year, one of their number would be doomed to turn into a wolf. If that person could only live for a year without tasting human flesh, he or she would return to human form; if not, he or she would remain a wolf forever. But to be a man turned wolf makes the hunger for human flesh a dreadful, and constant, temptation . . .

Ah, yes. Perhaps you have felt it too, by now: That very different sort of greed, aching in all your bones, at the root of every tooth. That itch beneath the skin, just where you can never quite reach. That song in your blood which calls out to the rising moon, dinning in your ears like some evil tide.

For we are all were-wolves here, make no mistake. Every parent who beats and rapes their own child, every man driven to eat his fellow's flesh—like a savage, though they most-times have better reason for it—by seasonal extremity. He, she, I, you; all of us who break the social compact by treating each other as something . . . less than human.

And the cry, the cry, echoing down unchanged throughout the ages: *It is not so, nor was not so, and God forbid that it should be so!*

But it *is* so. Is it not?

And still: *Calme-toi.* How could I possibly hurt you, *m'sieu*—an old woman like myself? Look at me. Look.

Yes, just that way.

Sit. Stay. *Assayez-vous*, each and every one of you, before I am forced to let my—worser—nature slip.

. . . better.

Ah, and now I recall how when I was but a gay girl like my poor Perrinette, still foolish enough to risk myself for trifles, I wore nothing but scarlet velvet . . . scarlet, so the stains would not show so badly. You understand.

Yet how times change, and how they do not. How do they never.

But I do not blame you for her death, any of you—oh no, not I. How could I, and not count myself a hypocrite? For I, of all people, should know how very difficult it is to refuse fresh meat when it presents itself, especially out here in this bleak and denuded frontier landscape. Out here, where hunger rules.

After all, I, too, have been known to prey on the unwary, in my time. I, too, have followed close behind travelling families, and used their love for one another to harry them to their doom. I, too, keep a cellar full of bones.

Yet I will give you this one thing for gift, *mesdames et messieurs* of The Poor Girl Taken By Surprise: This much, I will tell you for free. That there is more than one reason, traditionally, why a wolf who speaks—a wolf with human hands—should always be *burnt* rather than *eaten*.

You killed one of my children, and ate the other. But I do not begrudge you—since, in doing so, you have allowed yourselves to be eaten from inside-out by this same raging hunger that has always driven us, I and my kind, down all the long years before we came to this country, and after. In a way, you have *become* my children, my kin; *Tessdaluye* by nature, if not by name. And how could I harm my own kind, after all?

Well . . . easily enough, as I have explained already.

Nevertheless, I catch myself feeling generous, for now. For as a fellow hunter, I do so admire your arrangement here—this inn, sprung perpetually open like a trap disguised as providence; this fine, new trick of letting the little pigs come to be served and watching them serve themselves up, in turn. A steady stream of travelers lodging once, then moving on, and never being seen again: Only tracks in the snow, covered over before the moon next rises, and (here and there, in the underbrush) the rustle of soft paws following. With nothing left behind but the hard, dark scat of some unseen thing, so concentrated it must surely eat nothing but meat.

Oh yes indeed, *ça marche, absolutement. Ça ira.*

But never forget whose sufferance you live by from this moment on, curs. As last of my line, I am first in the blood here— alpha and omega, the aleph and the zed. And so you will come to my call, heel at my command, because I am—

—*ah, ça phrase?*

"Top dog."

You may even call me grandmother, if you wish.

IN THE POOR GIRL TAKEN BY SURPRISE: A COMMENTARY

FOLLOWING IN THE FEMINIST FOOTSTEPS OF Angela Carter, who famously revised the "Little Red Riding Hood" fable in her story "The Company of Wolves," Files enjoys revising the fairy tales and mythologies that are handed down to us, often in a manner that turns around the power relations that existed in the originals, exposing patriarchy for its flaws and oppressions. Carter's "Wolves" revised the Big Bad Wolf of the fairy tale into a werewolf and focused on female desire rather than victimization. Files plays some of the same keys on the literary piano, but in a distorted way that is more about familial vengeance and gendered justice than mere carnal lust. Files is far darker than

Carter, injecting these same archetypes with a savvy commitment to horror genre tropes, taking dark glee in turning our assumptions inside-out in a predatory or sadistic way, punishing patriarchy and the colonial impulses that are often attached to it, in the name of poetic justice.

In "The Poor Girl," Files brilliantly revises "Little Red Riding Hood" in an unforgettable way, bringing all the unique qualities of her writing to the party. For one thing, the language is playful with dialect and local diction, forcing us to side with the storyteller and interpret the invents she tells, even as she is unreliable in other ways. The title follows the naming traditions of indigenous cultures and gives us the name of a place, not a character, *per se*, as well, and this place—just like the story—is a set trap waiting for others to be "taken by surprise." The viewpoint character is a storyteller, yes, but also in her linguistically seductive manner she is presented to us as *trickster* figure, threatening to spring her own surprises at every turn as the tension builds. This trickster storyteller is just as disguised in her role as the Big Bad Wolf. That wolf—and the situation in which the audience finds themselves— is progressively unmasked in many ways that I won't spoil here— but in the end, a grand revelation of the nature of this place and the identity of the storyteller is unveiled. Suffice it to say that there is a powerful matriarchal context at work here—one that turns the tables upon the trappers and hunters—the woods-*men*—of the story.

What sharp teeth this story has. The better to eat them with.

—Michael Arnzen, PhD

SLICK BLACK BONES AND SOFT BLACK STARS

ALL GRAVES LOOK THE SAME, GENERALLY: SUNKEN or up-thrust, backdirt slightly looser than whatever lies around it, sometimes of a different color, a different composition. Anything that shows something's been scooped out and reapportioned, piled back in atop what lies beneath.

You start with trowel and probe, cleaning the surface near what you suspect is the grave's edge, thrusting the probe in as far as it'll go, then sniffing it for decomp. If you strike something soft, that's a find. Satellite photos also help, as do picks, shovels; Ken Kichi sets up nearby to run the electronic mapping station, charting the site's contours, eventually providing a three-dimensional outline of every body and its position when found, while Judy Moss—your usual dig partner—shares process photography duties with Guillaume Jutras, head of this particular Physicians for Human Rights forensic anthropology team. Their shutters buzz constantly like strange new insects in the oven-door heat, *snap-flash, snap-flash, whirrrr.*

And you, meanwhile—you're crouched down in the stench feeling for bones, finding rotten cloth, salt-stiff flesh.

The grave is humid, seawater-infused. Sand clings to everything, knitting with bone itself. At the very top, exposed to air and scavengers alike—crabs, birds—the bodies are slimy, broken down for parts, semi-skeletonized. Down farther, they're still fleshed, literally ripe for autopsy; those are the ones Jutras wants in the worst way. While down farther still . . .

Each stratum is an era, a span of time between massacres. The numbers vary: twos and threes, five-person groups at most, as opposed to the first and second layers' twenty-three. Deeper than that is where your particular skills will come most into play, differentiating one body's bones from another's, telling male from female, adult from child. You try not to feel bad about wanting to get down there as fast as possible, to see just how far down it all goes.

This tower of murder, thrown down, inverted. To you, it's a mystery, a challenge; to the people whose fragments it's made from—their relatives, at any rate—it's an obscenity, a disgrace. But you can't think about that, because it'll only slow you down, make you sloppy. Sentiment breeds mistakes.

Crouching down, feeling with both hands, gently but firmly. And saying silently to yourself, with every breath: *Keep working, keep quiet, keep sharp. Miss nothing.* Assuring them, at the same time: *Lie still, we're coming, finally. At long last.*

We're coming to bring you home.

You reached the island of Carcosa seven days ago, at 6:35 p.m. by your watch, only to find what looked like two suns staring down, one centered, the other offset—an upturned pupil, cataract-white, with a faint bluish tinge. *It's an optical illusion,* Jutras told you, during your conference-Skype briefing; *Everyone sees them. There's other things, too.*

Like what?

Just . . . things. It's not important.

(The clear implication: *You won't be there long enough for them to matter.* An assumption you don't question, since it suits you fine; you'll remember it later, though. And laugh.)

So yes, it's strange, though not unbearably so—no more so than the incredible heat or the smell accompanying it, rancid and inescapable, though you haven't even come near the dig site yet; the black beaches with their smooth-washed half-glass sand, the masses of shrimp-colored flowers and spindly nests of stick-insects creeping up every semi-vertical surface. Actually, all the colors are different here, just ever-so-slightly "off": the green laid on green of its grasses, fronds and vines isn't *your* green, not exactly. More like your green's occluded memory.

There's a wet woodsmoke tang to the air, like they've just doused a forest fire. Breathing it in gives you a languorous, possessive contact high—opium smoke mixed with bone-dust.

According to Jutras, the island—itself just the merest jutting peak of an underwater mountain-range ringed with black smokers, incredibly volatile—was once center-set with a volcano that exploded, Thera-style, its caldera becoming what's now known as "Lake" Hali. The quote-marks are because the lake itself is filled and re-filled with seawater brought in through a broken end-section that forms the island as a whole into a wormy crescent. Carcosa City occupies the crescent's midsection, its highest peak, while the two peninsulas formed by the crescent's horns almost overlap. The longer of the two is called Hali-joj'uk, "Hali-door" or "-gate," in the island's highly negotiable yet arcanely individual tongue. Wouldn't think there could be quite so many sub-dialects supported on an island whose entire population has never historically topped four hundred, and yet.

It's like every family has their own way of saying things, Jutras told you. *And they all understand each other, but they know you won't. That's why we have the interpreter.*

They don't trust folks from Away, Judy chimed in. *That's how they put it: there's them, and then there's Away. Everywhere else.*

Yeah, it's a serious Innsmouthian situation 'round these parts, Ken agreed. *Some inbred motherfuckers we're dealin' with, that's a certified fact.*

Ken, Jutras warned him, but Ken simply snorted.

What, man? It's just true. These people been marrying their cousins for a thousand years, by definition; cousins if they're lucky, and some years? I'm willing to take a bet the gene-pool maybe didn't stretch all that far. Like those Amish villages where the guys all have the same first name, and every dog's named "Hund."

Not a lot of cultural contamination on Carcosa, in other words, which is good in some ways, not so much in others. To cite another history of similar colonial isolation, in 1856—fifty-two years after being officially rediscovered by the British—Pitcairn Island, inhabited by the descendants of the H.M.S. *Bounty*'s mutineers, lost one hundred-percent of its population, gaining only sixteen of them back three years after. Since then, its numbers have fluctuated up and down—as high as two hundred and fifty in 1936, as low as forty-three in 1996. Yet numbers in Carcosa apparently remain steady, as though maintaining a strict death per birth replace-the-race policy . . . barring the occasional mass murder, that is.

Because that's what's brought you here, of course—like it always does, no matter where, no matter with who. Because this is your "business," the reckoning of mortality: to sex bones and extract DNA, to separate violent death covered up from more wholesome detritus, plague-pits or accidents or Acts of God alike, the dreadful human wreckage left behind whenever earth gapes wide, whenever the jungle sneezes up something that makes people cough themselves to death or sweat blood from every pore, whenever the sea rises up and bears away all in its path.

The whole island takes up approximately eighteen square miles, "lake" included. Nine of those take you from the airstrip to Hali-jo'juk, where the causeway to the dig awaits: Funeral Rock, yet one more island *inside* an island, a tiny chip barely a mile across, split off from the main rim back into Hali itself, a shelf of bare black crag-slopes cradling a black sand beach, which separates completely from the peninsula at high tide.

This is where it all happened; where no one will say how many of the island's otherwise rigidly-documented population were herded over no one will say how long a period of time, never to return. From what Judy and Ken have uncovered thus far, they think it must've begun long before the island was charted, let alone visited, and continued intermittently long after, with only the sheer numbers of the last mass-murder finally revealing the true nature of this particular "memorial" tradition at last . . . along with the fact that those taken to Funeral Rock for "burial" were not, strictly speaking, usually *dead* before the rocks and sand were thrown in on top of them.

All they know is, there's no telling how deep it goes down, Jutras told you, before you even started packing. *Which is why I need my best girl, Alice—to turn this around, ASAP.*

What's the hurry? you asked. *Top layer's the only one they can press charges with, right? I mean, the rest certainly proves a pattern of behavior, local prejudices, superstitions, maybe even religion-based motive . . . but in prosecutorial terms, just how useful is that?*

Jutras sighed. *Hard to say. It's a . . . weird situation, to say the least; slippery. Nobody knows who's responsible, or claims not to, so the authorities have just scooped up every able-bodied man within a certain radius; they don't have a jail, so they're holding them in the hospital's contagious ward.*

Because women *never kill* anybody, *right?* But since you both knew the answer to that one, you asked instead: *Who* are *the authorities in this case, exactly, anyway?*

Um... Wikipedia says the Hyades Islands, "a sub-archipelago thirty miles off the coast of East Timor," so—Indonesia, I guess? It's all pretty up in the air. A pause. *Point is, they don't even have cops here, let alone a court, so whoever does get charged with anything is going to have to be taken off-island for trial, and nobody's happy with* that *idea; the local garrison commander needs hard facts to keep Carcosa from blowing up around him, literally. Thus, us.*

You've worked with Jutras seven times before, all over. United Nations International Criminal Tribunal digs to start with, coordinated through The Hague—Darfur, then Cote d'Ivoire. Then on to smaller matters in far more obscure places, balancing corporate internal policing with volunteer work for far-flung, resource-poor communities. Carcosa definitely falls under the latter rubric, and also promises something the other sites most often don't: Mystery. Even back when you were finishing your internship in the Ontario Forensic Pathology Service, the final verdict on any case was almost never in doubt from the moment you first viewed the body on, be it murder, misadventure, or J-FROG (Just Plain Fuckin' Ran Out of Gas).

I've never heard of the Hyades, actually, you admitted, feeling stupid. *Carcosa either.*

Yeah, I'm with you there; had to look 'em up on the plane. But ours is not to reason, right?

And you might have disagreed with him, on that last part—should have, probably. But you were jet-lagged already, which never helps. One more dig didn't seem that big a deal.

Now here you are waist-deep in it, learning better.

Decomp clings to everything, in both senses of the word, just like the heat puts paid to modesty, prompting you and Judy to roll your coveralls to the waist over lunch, so you won't get corpse-rub in your food. Later, you'll pack today's "grave bra" into a plastic bag full of Woolite and choose tomorrow's from the rack it's been drying on in your hotel room closet. You buy seven new ones for every dig, color-coordinated by weekday, and leave them behind afterward, so stink-saturated they're only fit for burning.

The famous interpreter Jutras hired, Ringo Astur, sits with you under the canopy, waving flies away. Round-faced, eternally cheerful, chain-smoking imported cigarettes; his skin is the same color as Carcosa City's brick-work, a coral-tinged light brown, hair worn in short corn-rows. *How many today, Alice?* he asks you every noon and every night, eyes charm-crinkling, like it's some local version of *How* you *doin'?*

Three so far, Ringo. Why?

Oh, no reason. That's a lot, yes?

More and more, you want to tell him. More, and more, and *more . . .* Just what have these people been *doing* out here all this time, anyway?

Tell me about the other city, you say, instead. *The one from across Hali.*

Hm, he replies. *Well . . . that city's also named Carcosa, supposedly. It appears lake-center, where the volcano used to be—not always, not every night, but sometimes. Where the first Carcosa City stood once, before it dropped inside.*

Then there's a whole other Carcosa City under this lake?

A shrug. *So they say. And it appears, sometimes . . . we'd be closer to it here than back over there, if it did. They come down to the quay when it does, the people who live in it, and beckon, try to get us to row across.*

People live there?

Well, they look like people, yes, supposedly. They say they wear masks, those who've seen them.

You look down at your hands then, still stained from the grave; the sand's black tinge never seems to wash entirely off. Remembering one skull, its back crushed in with an axe-like implement, so fragile that when you threaded two fingers through its eye-sockets and a thumb through the nose-hole, it came apart in your hand—shed itself by sections even as you fought to keep it intact, yellow-grey bone sliding to sketch an entire fresh new face with palm-pink eyes and an unstrung, mud-filled mouth.

Unsurprising how easy they come apart, considering what you discovered on those top-layer excavations: Carcosans are full of cartilage, like sharks or octopi, with the proportion of actual collagen-poor bone to extensive net of tissue creepily small; all of them come out flexible yet springy, like osteogenesis imperfecta without the fracturing. You can see the signs from where you sit, in Ringo's bluish sclerae, his triangular face, that certain blurred malleability of feature which comes from most of your cranial plates simply not fusing, a head full of fontanelles and no joint left un-double. Once, in Carcosa City, you saw a not-exactly-small ten-year-old squeeze through a cat-door and pop out the other side laughing, to bound away into the brush.

Not enough bones in some ways, too many in others. And you're the only person, thus far, whoever seems to have thought of putting the extra ones together . . .

(But that's a private project, at least for now. You haven't even shown Jutras.)

It happens on two-sun days, mostly, around suns'-set, Ringo continues. *That's what they say. You look across Hali and there it is, all lit up, with the masks, and the beckoning. And then when you look up you see black stars high above, watching you.*

Who's this "they" you keep talking about, man? Ken yells at him, from over by the cooler. *I mean, you're related to basically everybody here, right? All those other Asturs? Old John-Paul-George Astur from the post office, Miss Sexy London Astur from the kelp farm? That dude Kilimanjaro Means We Couldn't Climb It Astur, from the boat repair?*

Don't be an arse, Ken, Judy tells him. *Jesus! What's it to you, anyhow?*

Now it's Ringo's turn to look down.

They don't talk to me much anymore, he says, finally. *Because I went Away. So I can't really ask them about any of it.*

You never saw it yourself, then? you find yourself asking.

Well… I did, yes. Once or twice, I think. I was young, a long time back. It was before, and Away—well, Away makes things like that hard to remember.

Ever try to go over?

No, no. That would be—that's a bad idea.

You nod, take a swig of water. Then something he said earlier comes back, prompting another question, before you can think better of it:

Closer over here… is that why people really came to Funeral Rock in the first place? So they'd have less of a way to row, if they wanted to make it to the other Carcosa?

Ringo looks at you hard for a long moment, not speaking. 'Til: *No,* he says, finally. *That's not why. They came to bury, or get buried. Like the King, in the story.*

… what story?

The King, Ringo tells you, once ruled in Other Carcosa City, before he was expelled and set adrift. He came from somewhere else entirely, far Away, farther than anywhere—came walking through their gates on foot one two-sun day, at suns'-set, and when asked to remove his mask as a gesture of friendship, claimed he didn't wear one.

Couldn't they tell? you ask, reasonably enough. But Ringo just shakes his head.

He looked... different, supposedly. Pale, yellow, with horns, all over—no one could think that was really his face; that's what they say. And yet... That's why the volcano blew up, you know. So they say.

Because of the King?

Because he wouldn't leave. So the people in Other Carcosa City made it happen, to make sure he did.

Wouldn't that have destroyed them, *too?*

Ringo shrugs. Concluding, after a beat: *Well, no, supposedly. They're—different.*

Later, back at camp, Judy maintains she's actually heard this same story a few times already, from other islanders. Which surprises the hell out of Ken, who—for all his bitching—probably hasn't tried talking to anybody without Ringo translating since he got here. Jutras easily confirms it, though, by pulling out an .mp3 he made on his phone of a woman (Miss Sexy London Astur?) telling the tale in Stage One Pidgin, the Malacca-Malay-inflected version of English Carcosans might've picked up from passing sailors, peppered with words you either can't hear or don't understand, your brain papering over the lacunae with whatever seems most contextually appropriate:

Many and many, one time there is to be being one [king] [magician] [warlord] [traitor], who is to be having all strength from the black pit of [stars] [salt] [silt], the bottom of every [hole] [mouth] [grave]. He is to be wearing no [mask] [face] [name]. He is to be being torn apart and ground down, thrown in seas, sunk deep, for fish to be eating. But then one time there are fish to be eating him, and islanders are to be eating the fish, with [pieces] [seeds] [bones] of him inside them. And then islanders are to be having children with [no bones] [no names] [no faces]...

You gulp, taste bile. *Jesus,* you say. *So... that's it, right? The motive. That's why?*

Classic Othering, with a fairytale spin, Jutras agrees. *I particularly like the whole Evil King deal that obviously keeps being trotted out every time these throwback genetic payloads pop up; you wait 'til it gets obvious, re-brand them as changelings spawned by the Enemy, then take 'em over to Funeral Rock and let "nature" take its course. "We 'had' to kill them, you see, because they weren't human, not really. Not like* us."

Look who's talkin', Ken mutters.

Judy frowns. *What I don't understand, though, is where this all came from, originally. The* idea *of this Evil King, of Other Carcosa City... all of it.*

"Away," I guess, Jutras replies. *Except... no, they were doing this long before anybody else ever came by here, so—some sort of primal phobia about the sea, maybe: All that water, everything underneath it, the earthquakes, all the instability. It has to be somebody's fault.* A pause. *That's the theory, anyway. Except it's hard to say, because, uh... nobody will say.*

You can't possibly believe—

Of course not, Alice, but they *believe it. Enough to kill twenty-three children, and God knows how many more...*

Now it's your turn to nod, to stare. And reply, eventually:
. . . I should show you something, probably.

Looking at what you've so neatly laid out on a canvas tarp in a shallow trench three feet from the grave's lip, elements-sheltered under a fresh new tent, Jutras says nothing, just stares down. You don't blame him, exactly; did it yourself, the first time you finally thought to stop and breathe. Now the words spill out in a similar rush, barely interrupted, monologue paced to an adrenaline rush tachycardia beat, so fast it barely seems to be *your* voice you're both hearing say these things, with complete declarative confidence— the same authoritarian, spell-casting rhythm that renders truth from lies, makes fiction into fact, simply by stating even the most ridiculous-sounding things out loud.

You study him closely as you speak, too, just in case: strain to read every minor shift, each muscle-twitch, each spasm. Almost as though you think that at some point his own eye-whites are going to turn blue, jaw and temples deforming, as the planes of his skull soften 'til they slide to form someone else's face entirely.

Remember how Ken kept saying these people weren't like us? Well, asshole that he is, turns out he's actually right. The adult human body has two hundred and six bones. These . . . have more. Best approximate total: just over three hundred and fifty, like a human infant, almost as though their bones never fused properly— and three times the normal amount of cartilage, so it doesn't much matter that they didn't. Like they were never meant *to; like they were* supposed *to reach adulthood able to squeeze themselves easily through spaces that'd break a normal adult human's neck.*

Also, the reason it's "just over" is because it seems each body's inevitably got two duplicates of one particular bone . . . except it's never the same one. This woman has two fibulae. This man has two second thoracic vertebrae. This child has two mandibles—must've made it hard to talk, especially since the second one is adult-sized. It's like God was smuggling a whole other person into Carcosa, hidden inside these people's bodies.

But—what can I say; I guess everybody caught on.

Oh, and now that we've reached the bottom—did that yesterday—you know how many corpses are in this grave, exactly? Three hundred and fifty.

Plus one.

It's that "plus one" Jutras' looking at right now, the nameless guest at this carrion feast, painstakingly pieced together in anatomical explode-a-view. On its own it'd seem like some drunk pre-med student practical joke, a botched bastardization transformed together from three or more skeletons at once: spine articulated like a boa constrictor's, ribs everywhere, even in its limbs; skull like a Rubik's helmet, slabbed and fluted and interlocking, a puzzle-box with a million solutions but no answers. The fact that it proved surprisingly easy to assemble is the least of your worries, a strangeness so trivial it's barely worth sparing the energy to consider . . . not when there's so much more about the whole exercise to avoid thinking about at all, in retrospect.

How long has that mold been growing on it? Jutras asks.

What mold?

He points, and you finally see it: grey as the bones themselves, furry. Hard to tell what you thought it was before, if you even registered its existence—moisture? Condensation?

I . . . don't know. Why?

. . . no reason.

But he's already backing away, step by step; peeling the flap without looking, shimmying himself free. You hear him take a long, shaky breath, almost like he's tensing against nausea, trying not to vomit. His walkie gives an almighty crackling howl.

There's something happening, he says, at last, after a hushed, one-sided conversation. *In the city. I have to go.*

And a minute later, it's just you and the bones again.

Jutras is out of contact for most of the next day, which means he isn't there for the undersea quake that rattles the island. Minor as tremors go, the epicenter's out by the black smoker ring that keeps Carcosa's shores so fertile, so teeming with fish and kelp-forests; closer to Carcosa City than Funeral Rock, thankfully, so the back-slop doesn't do much more than submerge the causeway far faster and for far longer than expected. You didn't even notice it yourself until you came out of the tent and found Ken and Judy on the horn with Jutras, yelling at him about being stuck on-site for the night until the causeway emerges again. Said prospect bothers you less than it should, but that could just be sheer exhaustion. Who knew watching mold grow could be so draining.

What *does* bother you—silencing Ken and Judy as well—is what Jutras finally tells you, when he gets a word in edgewise: The quake brought in a mini-tsunami that cracked the hospital apart, shearing off the wall of the contagious ward. In the confusion, most massacre suspects cut and ran, disappearing into a sympathetic web of back-rooms, basements, cliff-caves, and other assorted hidey-holes. Surprisingly few injuries amongst the military guards, and all from natural causes rather than any sort of hostile action, but all of you can read between the lines: the garrison is confused and demoralized from the bottom up, perhaps even fixing to cut and run, and the islanders themselves . . . well, they aren't happy. To say the least.

They've heard what you're doing here, Ringo tells you, after Jutras signs off. *Putting the King back together—that's why this happened. They want to stop you.*

Ken snorts. *So these dudes in jail, what, called up a wave and surfed on out of there? C'mon, man. Army'll pick 'em up by tomorrow; this place ain't big enough to hide in, not for long.*

You don't know that. You don't know anything about us.

I know enough, man.

No. Ringo shakes his head, visibly struggling to keep polite. *It's . . . not safe for you here, not now, any of you. You should go.*

Go where? you ask, waving Ken silent, while Judy hugs herself. *Where should we go, Ringo?*

Without hesitation: Away, *of course. And take me with you, when you do.*

Though you're hardly a mycologist or sapro-phytologist by trade, anyone who works enough decomp learns to ID the key fungal players soon enough. The stuff that's growing over "the King"'s bones still doesn't match anything you recognize: too tough, spreading too fast, especially without an identifiable nutrient-source. You take a moment to look up the region on your tablet, looking for a local flora-and-fauna rundown, and pause at Wikipedia's disambiguation page for "Hyades." There are four entries: the islands, the band, the Greek mythological figures, and a star cluster in the constellation Taurus.

You look up in the dusk light, out across the lake. The "twin suns" sink toward the horizon in a blurry shimmer. A mirage, an illusion; the same thing that makes the suns look almost bluish-white, rather than red-gold. So Ringo says. You look back down to your tablet, and click on the entry for the star cluster. Thinking, as you do, about articles some of your geekier friends have sent to you, essays about such things as static wormholes, and equipotential space-time points; quantum tunneling, black branes and folded space, negative energy densities.

The Hyades cluster is more than six hundred million years old, far older than most such stellar groups, a survivor of the aeons by orbiting far from galactic center. At least twenty of its stars are A-type white giants, with seventeen or eighteen of them thought likely to be binary—double-star—systems. It appears in the *Iliad* on the shield that Hephaestus made for Achilles, and is named for the daughters of Atlas, who wept so hard over the death of their brother Hyas they eventually became the patron stars of rain.

Twilight deepens, and your tablet's glow increases in the growing dark. But your shadow grows sharp to one side, beyond what the tablet could illuminate, and you look up once more.

Above the center of the lake, where the volcano exploded centuries ago, lights glow in a scattered matrix of green, blue, gold, and red, clear and cold. The darkness between them seems to outline shapes—structures, blocks, towers. They're hard to look at, defying your eyes' focus almost painfully. Can't tell if the blur is distance, or atmosphere mirage, or the wake of motion too fast to follow. The blue-green, poisonous light of the setting suns behind it twists your stomach. You feel the whole thing *pulling*, physically, like a hook in the gut: some second force of gravity, pressing you toward the lake and the place you know isn't there, *can't* be there—

—not because it isn't real, but because it's somewhere else. Some utter, alien elsewhere, so far away its light is older than your species.

It's that pull, that nausea and that disbelief, which keeps you from hearing the tumult until it's too late. Distracted by Other Carcosa City's spectacular appearance, you simply haven't noticed the boats' approach, silent and sure—pontooned sea-canoes, anchoring themselves at Funeral Rock's base so their passengers can shinny up the handhold-pocked cliff and emerge through those cave-entrances you never even knew were there, almost under your feet.

A burst of bullets, muzzle-flare in the night, and Ringo's already up, hauling on your arm: *Alice, come, come on, Alice—now, now, now, they're here! Leave everything!*

But—Ken, Judy, Jesus, Ringo! What about . . .

Too late, come on! *We have to* go—

Across Hali, behind Other Carcosa City's gleaming shoreline, you can just glimpse the "real" capitol going up in flames, a series of controlled explosions. Is one of those Jutras' field-office, the garrison, the sea-plane that brought you here? Over near the grave, meanwhile, Ken's scrabbling for his data, uploading frantically; one shot catches him in the shoulder, another in the upper back, sending him straight over the lip. You can hear him thrashing down below, desperately trying to cover himself in enough sand-muck to turn invisible. Ringo pulls you headlong while the attackers rush the camp, smashing and tearing, hurling equipment and evidence alike into the sea. Ripping up the tents, they riddle every prepped body-bag they uncover with yet more gunfire, as though they think something might be hiding in there.

Good thing I moved him, you find yourself thinking. *Good thing, good thing . . .*

Ringo drops to his knees, dragging you along with him; your knees jolt, painfully. *In here, Alice,* he says. *Come on! This one goes out the opposite side—we can swim, they'll never see us.*

Swim? Where the hell to?

Other Carcosa City, of course; no one will expect it. Can't you see them, beckoning?

But: That's just a bit too much crazy to stomach, even now. So here you pull back, wrenching yourself free, even as Ringo worms his way slickly down into the earth, gone in seconds—you'd never make it anyway, is what you tell yourself. The gap's far too narrow, too twisting; you'd simply lodge fast, bruised and scraped and strained to breaking, to die crushed like a bug. You let him go instead, whispering, *Goodbye.*

Why? Judy yells from behind you, uselessly, drawing another burst. *Why, why?*

Because some things are meant to stay buried, a voice replies, from deep inside.

Then: Spotlights stab down out of the growing dusk, helicopter rotors roaring, as speakers filter what must be orders far past the point of comprehensibility. More gunfire strafes the camp, this time vertically; Judy's head explodes outright, GSW damage simultaneously shock-hammering away one half of your body in a series of consecutive hits to forearm, shoulder, hip, thigh. The downdraft wraps you in already-torn tent-fabric like a plastic bag shroud, momentum rolling you straight into the scrub where you stowed "the King"'s reassembled body, so you sprawl almost nose to whatever it uses for a nose with it.

No pain, simply shock, cold and huge enough to sharpen your observational skills to inhuman levels. The not-fungus has finished its work. The creature's skin is black everywhere but its pallid mask of a face, slick and soft, oily to the touch, almost warm; that's your blood it's soaking up, spongelike, as if every pore is a feeding orifice, swelling with the sacrifice.

And its massive, horned head turns, yellow eyes cracking open. Locking upon yours.

I am here, it tells you; *Look across the lake, where my city rises, and watch us beckon. You have done me great service, bringing me back into this world.*

Now: Be not afraid, lie still, lie quiet. Your long wait is over.

Beyond the hovering 'copter, those two suns sink down, white-blue turning red, filling Hali's caldera with false lava. And when you slump over onto your back, looking up again by sheer default, you see stars: Soft black stars, almost indistinguishable, in a black, black sky.

The King lays one scaly hand on your brow, lightly. Almost affectionately.

I am coming, he promises, *to take you home.*

Slick Black Bones and Soft Black Stars: A Commentary

WHILE THIS STORY MAY AT FIRST CONFOUND readers who are unfamiliar with Robert Chambers's "The King in Yellow," in my view it teaches everything readers might need to know about that story cycle, which has inspired many a dark fantasist over the past century-plus, most notoriously H.P. Lovecraft and others interested in the subgenre that we now term "cosmic horror." It's a brilliant contribution to the mythos. Everything from the reference to twin suns and black stars to Carcosa signal to the reader that this story plays with Chambers's concepts, but it radically rewrites the cycle by approaching it in a manner akin to modern "folk horror." I read this piece as critical of colonization, brilliantly focusing on a female scientist seeking escape from the constructs of the "real" world. (For more analysis, jump to my critical piece featured later in this collection, "Why Gemma Files Matters.")

—Michael Arnzen, PhD

Venio

WATCH OUT.

I'm going to tell you about something, and then ... you'll know. You won't be able to *un*-know, or forget why you should want to. And even if you decide you don't believe it now, you'll still have thought about it long enough to make that call, so it'll still be too late. Because now it knows you know, it'll be able to find you. To home in on you.

Just like it did with me.

Sometimes, a door is enough, open or otherwise. Or an empty moment, an empty page.

An empty head.

I remember the night my group and I first played the game that led us here, the Shut Door Sessions. It was all about imagination, or the lack of it.

We were writers, you see, supposedly. Desperate to be. And yes, I know the received wisdom, thank you very much—how you can fix *bad* writing, but you can't fix *no* writing. How nothing you put down in words is ever going to match that gleaming, awe-inspiring thing you glimpse at the back of your head, so you might as well just let it come as it comes and try to make it better later on. Try not to fixate on how the gold you had, just before you started trying to hammer it into words, somehow seems to have turned entirely to shit, an alchemical working in reverse: albedo up out of nigredo and back on down into nigredo again, hi ho, hi ho.

Always seeking the same goal, all of us, with no real hope of achieving it: something fresh, something new, something real—*unique.* The impossible fucking dream.

We'd all been there. We'd all spent most of our writing lives there, high school awards or university chapbook-publishing aside. And we'd still be there now, still stuck on the stories we weren't qualified to wrestle from dream to page, if we'd never started playing that game.

Christ, how I wish we'd never started playing that game.

Here's how it works: You each get a piece of paper, blank, lined or unlined, depending on what works best for you. You each get a pen. It can't be your own pen or a piece of paper from your own notebook, if you have one; the work has to be done physically, not electronically—no tablets, no laptops, no phones. *And I don't give a shit about how your ADD means you can't spell without spell-check, Trevor, this isn't* school. *I'm not taking marks off for presentation.*

Four people around a four-person table, the sort made for family dinners. One person per cardinal direction with just enough elbow room to scribble without hurting each other, assuming you're all similarly-handed. And at the top of each page you draw a door, any sort, so long as it's shut.

Draw a door, a shut door, locked if it must be, and look at it. Look at it for as long as you must before you can write down exactly what'd be behind it, if it opened.

And which of us was it who first got the idea that grew into this weird-ass prompt turned ritual? Oh, that would be Leah, obviously. Little Ms. "The Voices in My Head Aren't Talking to

Me Directly This Week" herself, the queen of pants versus plot, always puking out stuff in seemingly unrelated chunks before stringing it together afterward and telling people her characters told her how to do it. The woman whose whole idea of outlining is to basically throw a pack of Tarot cards in the air, turn them over at random once they hit the ground, and see what happens.

Leah and I had once been together in the sharing-a-bed sense, as opposed to the simply sharing-an-apartment one: met in first year, moved in together by third year, then broke up the year after graduation only to discover there was nowhere to move within public transit distance that wouldn't cost twice as much rent as we were already paying. Which is how we still came to be "together" when she started the Shut Door Sessions, two roommates turned exes pretending we could actually be some variety of friends even after what happened . . . happened.

Such a cliché, too, all said and done, especially for two people so deeply engaged in trying to avoid clichés like the plague. One of those uncomfortable breakups where you don't really want each other's company any more but have far too much in common to avoid each other without making a scene. I mean, nobody *wants* to be the Crazy Ex from Hell, do they? The bitch, the asshole, the one who ruins things for everyone else. Don't want to make your other friends unhappy, assuming you have some. So why throw the few friends you've already got away over something as negligible as mere post-physical entanglement heartbreak?

—⁂—

Just play along, guys, okay? No matter how silly it seems. Look at your door, let your eyes unfocus. Relax. Breathe deep and open yourselves up.

Just open yourselves up and wait to see what comes through.

Leah's voice in Yuri's living room that first night, excited enough to turn just a bit breathless, the way I'd heard it so many times before, albeit under very different circumstances. Which maybe explains why I was not only willing but eager to go along with this ridiculous plan of hers—chase the monkey down the monkey-track one more time, in hot pursuit of a truly inventive creativity I already suspected I had never really possessed. I'm talking about the ability to see something lurking inside a block of mental marble and free it with just a few pen-strokes. Craft a sentence clean as a bone over and over again, then hook them together into the skeleton of something never seen before.

My door was featureless, graphic, almost hieroglyphic—I'm a writer, not a visual artist. A bare rectangle with a small circle inside, halfway down the right-hand post . . . a handle, probably smooth brass, or maybe one of those old glassine diamonds with a bit of paint-slop left down around the part that rotates, turning left to pull tongue from lock and open inward to reveal—

"The part that rotates," hell . . . I really should know what that thing's called, right? Considering my profession.

The door, and what's behind it. What's behind your door? See it, guys. Write it down.

Write it down, then tell me.

And now you want to stop, I'll bet—to pull out before you go much further, let alone the whole, full way with me. But you can't, can you? You need to know what you won't be able to stop thinking about, if you do.

Besides which: it's already too late, really. I mean, you've already read this far.

Haven't you?

Here's what I wrote, that first time:

A dark road, or what looks like one. No moon and no horizon. Hard to see where the ground blends with the sky, but as it comes toward the door-frame it starts looking porous, tactile. Tiny holes or tiny stones? Gravel? A bed of gravel on either side of two long, dull gray lines with lighter lines between them like a ladder on the ground or maybe train tracks, away into the distance. Trees on either side? Shadows, spiky, overhanging. They switch back and forth on the tracks, no noise, but if there was it would be rustling. Distant. A high and a lonely wind. Nothing else.

Breathing in, breathing out. Resisting the urge to check my watch. Listening to the scratch of other people's pens around me—trying not to picture Leah with her tongue-tip caught between her teeth, bottom lip a little furled to show darker pink inside pale lipstick. Trevor scribbling hard, like he's fighting the alphabet. Yuri humming. Trying not to recognize the tune.

The posts are darkening, shadow spreading outward. A black thickening at the threshold, like drool.

(I wanted to stop then too, believe me. That early on. Before I'd even seen . . . anything.)

Another tick, a half-breath, barely tasted. And then—

Now a sense of something changing in the furthest section: a dot, dark separating from dark. Thinning as it moves closer, paced like a man's stride, not quick, not slow. Steady. Taller now. The track isn't completely straight like it seemed, there's a rise, and he's moving up it, cresting it. Very tall now, very, in a long dark coat like the song. Head down, hood up. Movement around the knees, pump of muscle and flutter of wind. The coat is black. His face is pale, obscure. Pitted? Hair down across the eyes? Chin pointed?

Nothing to stop him. Nothing that can *stop him.*
I don't know where he's going. Coming.
Coming <u>HERE</u>?

My hand formed the word, the question mark, <u>HERE</u> plus a squiggle above a dot. Underline swooping up into two-part quirk done so fast it scarred the page, barely separated, ink bleeding into ink.

Shut it again, and fast, I remember thinking, breath hissing back out like a stomach-punch, *just do it slam it lock it. Just shut shut* shut the fucking door.

"*Annnd* done," Leah chimed in overtop, cheerily. "Pens down, guys. Let's see what we've got."

I remember sitting back, flipping my paper as I did so, like I was afraid what might come out of it. Then seeing Leah point at Trevor, who winced, and started reading.

"Behind my door, um, what I see is, like … a long dark road," he began, flat and halting, eyes squinched as if having trouble with his own words. "Or a bunch of train tracks? One track, going off through a forest, uh … and it's really hard to see where it goes because the trees are all, like, jam-packed in on either side—"

Across the table, Yuri snorted. "You fucking kidding me?" he asked, glaring at Trevor.

Leah, still breathless: "Uh—no crit until we're all finished, please … "

"Oh, seriously? When joker here just read mine upside-down and copied it, instead of making up his own? *Real* mature, T."

Trevor flushed. "Am I supposed to know what the fuck he's talking about?"

"Guys," said Leah. "*Guys.*" But Yuri was off again, as he so often was during these workshop attempts: he was an old-school Asimov fan who believed anything other than Ass-In-Chair-Hands-On-Keyboard was self-indulgent time-wasting and didn't think much of Trevor's too-obvious eagerness to try anything Leah proposed. Nor had he ever stinted at saying so, bluntly. If anything was a surprise this time, it was the uncharacteristic ferocity with which Trevor came back at him, for once; within minutes both were on their feet yelling at each other, with Leah shrinking between, her feeble efforts at mediation completely silenced.

Nobody noticed me, at the time, picking up Trevor's page and scanning it. Then Yuri's. After which, I got up and left, leaving my own scribble on the table without saying anything.

I don't think anybody noticed that for a while, either.

"Kris?" Hand on my shoulder, light, tinglingly familiar. It took some effort not to roll toward the touch for a kiss. "You awake?"

"Am now," I muttered. The bedroom was dark, but it wasn't like Leah needed the lights to know her way around. "Sorry. Should've said goodbye."

"No, no. I understand." The hand withdrew; a small, compact weight settled itself on the bed, carefully distant. After a moment, paper crackled. "I, um—I thought you might want this." And there it was, thrust without warning in front of my face. My Shut Door exercise. I had to stifle the urge to rip it from her hands and tear it into shreds.

In hindsight I don't think that would have helped. But I still wish I had. Instead, I just took it, levered myself upright and slipped it into my bedside table drawer. Leah watched, wide eyes glinting in the dark.

"Is that really what you wrote?" she asked.

"What do you think?"

I hate how you do that, I remember her shouting at me. *Dodge questions by asking more questions, you always put everything back on me!* But she surprised me. Not saying anything, she shuffled close enough to reach the bedside lamp, turned it on, then gave me another piece of paper. I stared at her. She just nodded at the paper and gazed back.

Her door was pure Leah: a neat little sketch of opened gates with arching tops and angular runes above them, Tolkien's Mines of Moria entrance in miniature. Below that, her handwriting reeled across the page in the familiar chicken-scratches. Reading it had always, always been an effort in squinting patience and guesswork . . . until now. *Railroad tracks off into the dark,* it began. *I see them through the trees. A night with no moon, and he comes walking . . .*

I didn't need to read the rest, any more than you need to read it now. All sleepiness was gone, though I couldn't have told you what replaced it. Fear didn't seem like the right word. It felt more like prickly queasiness. Like nothing I'd ever felt.

"Trevor didn't copy Yuri," I said, roughly. "Neither did you. Right?"

Leah shook her head. "I—I thought, for just a minute, that he might have. I mean, if he was really desperate enough to impress you, then maybe he—"

"Impress *me?* I thought he was hung up on you."

That got a smile I hadn't seen in a long time; something caught in my throat. Leah shook her head. "God, Kris, you never could pick up on that kind of thing." The smile faded. "No, he was too angry. Which means it was real. Which means . . . " She let out a shaky breath. "I also got this word in my head," she said, without segue. "Like I was hearing it from far away. An echo of an echo. Something—something Latin, I think."

"I didn't know you knew Latin."

"I don't, it just—sounded that way to me. Like a Roman name from *Asterix*, or something." She stopped by the door, arms folded, half-turned away. I couldn't see her eyes any more.

"Are you okay?" I blurted, before I caught myself. We'd stopped asking each other that sort of thing. But all I got was a dull shrug.

"Sure." A deep breath; a sidelong look. "I don't think the exercise worked tonight, though."

"Probably... better not to do it again, then," I answered carefully.

"Probably."

So much that could have been said, in that look. None of it anything we could say. Nothing that would have made a difference, even now.

"Good night, Kris," she said, and left.

Not a forest, this time. Flat, open prairie, an achingly wide night sky overhead; stars like spilled salt, crusting purple clouds. I stood amid swaying, whispering plants that might have been corn, or wheat, or savannah grass. A black shadow painted a depthless rectangle before me on the plain; I could smell the barn's wood mold and wet hay, undercut with dead mice and desiccated cow shit. A road cut across the plain past me, straight as a laser beam. The full moon blazed.

Made it all the easier to see.

The walker was farther away, tiny, only a smudged speck of moving black where the road disappeared into the invisible horizon. No way to tell where he was looking, though his shape inched slowly but evenly down the road's dead center, as if he was staring straight ahead. But I knew he knew I was there. Just as I knew why he wasn't hurrying. What need? He knew I couldn't move.

It should have taken a long time for him to reach me. Maybe it did. Time slips around in dreams, we all know that. But he didn't change course even as he approached. Hooded, black-cloaked, nothing but shadow under the cowl; his head didn't angle toward me. He wasn't even particularly *tall*—maybe six feet, if that. And the cloak draped and flowed like a perfectly normal human was wearing it. Even his movement looked like an ordinary walk. A steady, slightly-too-rhythmic walk, but a walk.

And . . . he was passing me by. Not even turning to look.

I had half an instant to feel a surreal mix of giddy relief, bemused shock and even something like indignation, like part of me wanted to yell *Is that* it?! But then—

I want to tell you the word he told me: the word that sounded right in my ear, despite the distance between us; the word spoken at a nearly normal volume, calm, quiet, without rancor, without haste. But the explosion of sheer terror it detonated inside me erased it even as I heard it—a trauma so huge it blotted itself out in the instant of its own creation, the way the mind discards any pain too huge to process. Like when a tooth's pulled without freezing, or a bone breaks; when you knock the wind out of yourself, when you get a concussion. You know it happened, and you know you never want it to happen again, but . . . that's all, that's it. Nothing else.

Just the scar where it's been.

At some point I realized I was awake. My mouth and throat felt dry, and dizziness lingered; I must have been hyperventilating. Had I screamed? Leah would have come running to check on me if I had. Unless—I checked the alarm clock and groaned. No, she was long gone to work by now. I made myself get up, shower, and get dressed, even though my shift at the bookstore didn't start for hours.

The apartment was unnervingly quiet. I did what little busywork I could find, which didn't take long. And then, without letting myself think about it, I went into Leah's room and sat down on the bed.

I hadn't allowed myself to do this in nearly two years. This had been the room we'd shared, while we were together—I'd taken the spare bedroom afterward because I had far less stuff to move out; I'd never collected anything like her vast array of kitsch, knickknacks, and tschotschkes, like the horde of ceramic monkeys still taking up an entire shelf or the rows of unused Sacred Heart candles littering her dresser. Boxes and boxes of odds and ends, strewn along the windowsill. The closet stuffed to bursting with clothes. And her smell, still in the air, without any need to press my face into the pillow.

You had to look close to see what was missing. Beside the stereo, the stack of CDs was half the height it had once been. A sparsely-filled bookshelf, slightly bent, as if it had long held up a much heavier weight. A protruding nail on the wall where a picture had hung, the sort of thing everybody reminds themselves to get around to removing and never remembers. But if you didn't think to look, you wouldn't notice. You might think nobody else had ever slept here.

Maybe it was anger that made me get up and go to the second box from the right on her windowsill, the only one you needed to know the trick to open. Fingernails in the right hidden slots: slide, twist, press, *click*. I dug out the notepad and pencil that Leah had showed me, the pad where I knew she wrote down her dreams. And for the first time in two years I sat down and started reading.

Nothing about me, which was both relief and disappointment. The usual surreal nonsense. One surprising scene about Yuri, of all people—I'd always known Leah's tastes were wider than mine but hadn't thought she felt anything for him beyond friendship. Journeys, conversations, images clearly plucked out and set aside for some future poem—

I turned to the last page and stopped. She'd written something down here… but it had been utterly obliterated by a black charcoal smear scribbled so forcefully onto the paper that the sheet itself felt warped under my fingers. I tilted it back and forth under the light, trying to make something out, but gave up when my eyes started to hurt.

Then a better idea came to mind. I flipped to the next page, took the pencil, and began delicately shading light gray over the paper. The impression of the word bloomed up in white against the gray, gouged into the pulp; almost, but not quite, too faint to see.

(*Like I was hearing it from far away. An echo of an echo. Something Latin, I think…*)

On her desk, Leah had left her computer open and running, as she always did. One Google search and the answer was there in front of me. It was, indeed, Latin. My face felt numb.

Venio.

I am coming.

I begged off sick from my shift, waited for Leah to get home and told her what I'd found. I was a little surprised she didn't get angry—violation of her privacy was one of the few things that normally set her off—but I guess both of us knew we were beyond that now. We called the guys. Trevor, surprise surprise, was perfectly willing to meet tonight even on this short notice; Yuri took some persuading, but finally agreed, and even offered his living room again.

Once Yuri had finally gotten it through his head that no, this wasn't some kind of practical joke, he practically went berserk; it was the most excited I'd ever seen him. "Don't you *get* it, Kris?" he raved, striding around the room. "We've actually achieved something *paranormal* here! Subconscious telepathic communication, at least—or maybe we actually *contacted* something! A spirit, a ghost, whatever..."

"Well, you know, it could also be—" Trevor began.

Yuri didn't listen. "We have to do this again. Now we all know what to concentrate on, maybe we can make contact consciously. God! I should record this. Let me get my phone." He sprinted out and was back in a second, setting up his phone on a sideboard by the dining room table. Trevor looked at me helplessly.

"Yuri. *Yuri.*" I had to raise my voice. He blinked at me. "Yuri, we didn't do this to convince you to keep going with it. We want it to *stop.*"

Yuri stared. "That's ridiculous," he said after a moment, in a perfectly level voice. "That's *stupid.* That's like Alexander Fleming throwing out his moldy petri dishes without checking them first. Look, we're not calling up Captain Howdy on a Ouija board here. We're confirming whether we're sharing the same mental experiences. That's *all.* Besides, if you want it to stop, doesn't it make more sense to finish it? Wrap it up, bring it to a conclusion, whatever it is?"

Trevor cleared his throat. "I, um... I gotta say, I kind of don't want to leave it hanging either. You're... you're supposed to face this stuff, I think. That's what Dr. Tallan always told me."

I turned to Leah for backup. The look on her face was like a slap. My fists knotted. "Fuck's sake, don't tell me you're buying this," I snapped at her.

She swallowed but didn't flinch. "Kris, I'm sorry," she said in a small voice. It sounded almost exactly like the way she'd said *I'm sorry* two years ago, when she'd first asked me to move out. "But I don't want to have that dream again. Do you?"

No, but—The words disintegrated in my mouth, leaving nothing behind.

Yuri clapped his hands, as if that had settled it. "Okay, then. Let's do this. Everybody, get a piece of paper from someone else; Leah, give me your pencil, I'll get pens for the rest of us..." Of course, he'd remembered the procedure exactly, even while he was scoffing. Before I knew it, we were all seated around the table again, and Trevor, at Yuri's order, was setting a timer on his own phone under the steady stare of Yuri's camera lens. Yuri took his seat, practically rubbing his hands in glee. "You know how this goes, guys. Draw the door. Concentrate on it. And open yourself up to see what comes through." He nodded to Trevor. "Go."

Trevor started the timer, then bent his head to his paper. So did Leah and Yuri. I put my pencil on the paper but sat still, fully intending to draw nothing, write nothing. Okay, I'd scribble the pencil around meaninglessly a little, just to make it look good, but—

My mouth dried.

From what I'd been sure were completely random muscle movements, the cartoon-simple shape of the door—rectangle, tiny circle—had somehow emerged. I couldn't take my eyes from it. My hand cramped; my fingers hurt; my forearm ached. The pencil scribbled across the page. The door seemed to be blurring in and out.

Not real, I thought fuzzily. *Think of something real, but faraway. If he's coming to where he thinks you are, show him something different. Send him on.* I tried to conjure up places in my mind that I knew I'd never seen, even to recognize on TV: Boise, Cleveland, Saskatoon. Minsk. Aachen. Beijing. Locations that were nothing more than a name and a vague direction.

But the problem is that the more you try to imagine what's too unfamiliar to conceive, the more your own familiarities snap into place in the gaps, like a default reflex you can't control. The nameless city becomes your own city; a shapeless street becomes a road you know. Any building becomes your building… or your friend's. The corridor becomes an all-too-recognizable hallway. And as the shadows pour down that hallway, surrounding the silently walking figure, its hand lifting to the door to knock, the more your head wants to turn from the paper door to the real one, even while part of you is desperately screaming not to look up, not to look, not to—

Trevor's phone went off in a flurry of electronic chimes. I jumped. Across the table, Leah looked like she wanted either to burst into tears or throw up. Yuri shook his head, seeming to snap awake. "Whoa," he said. "Okay, I'll read mine first, then we—"

A knocking came at the door. Not loud, not heavy-handed; polite, almost diffident. Yuri scowled. "Fuck *me*, go the fuck away," he muttered. When the knocking came again, he repeated himself, this time in a shout: "Fuck *off*, asshole!"

The knocking only continued. Yuri rolled his eyes. I stared at him, trying to get enough breath into my lungs to ask him: Couldn't he *see* it? The shadow, coagulating thickly around the edges of his front door, like tar seeping through cardboard? Couldn't he feel the cold in the air? But I couldn't even get my hand to move as he rose from his chair and strode toward the door. Leah was whimpering. Trevor stared at me like a kid waiting for his parents to explain something he didn't understand. Yuri reached the door, grabbed the knob, twisted it, and flung it open.

There was nobody there. And simultaneously all the shadow, all the chill, it was all gone. I could move again. Breathed easily. The absence of fear felt almost like being drunk. Yuri looked down the outside hall, then blew out an exasperated breath. "Well, that was—" he began, turning around.

The doorway behind him went night-black. Something reached out of the darkness behind him, seized his shoulder, and pulled. Yuri flew backward like a stuntman on a wire and vanished, the void that swallowed him gone in the same instant. The door hung open. The hallway was empty.

I sat there still, same position. Couldn't move a muscle. Leah was the one who went white. Trevor was the one who vomited.

I don't think it ever occurred to any of us to call the police. We couldn't have told them anything they'd believe, obviously. But worse than that, we couldn't have told them anything *we'd* believe. Every 911 call ever made boils down to one of just two messages: *Help me please* or *It's not my fault*; both at once, more often than not. Problem is, neither of those were true. They still aren't.

Nobody could help Yuri, any more than they could help us. And it *was* our fault.

Trevor cleaned up his sick while Leah had a sobbing breakdown on the couch. I replayed what Yuri's phone had recorded, over and over, but the lens hadn't been pointed toward the front door. Again and again, the knocking came; Yuri scowled, swore, shouted, then got up and walked out of frame as the three of us stared after him; his last, almost-inaudible half sentence; and then, the reaction—Leah swaying, me frozen, Trevor doubling over. It was nearly hypnotic. I only came out of it when Trevor tapped me on the shoulder and told me he was walking me and Leah home.

We had to leave the apartment door unlocked, of course.

I don't remember much of that walk. I barely remember Trevor in the door of our apartment, insisting that it was no problem at all to crash on our couch, and Leah pushing him out, sounding too tired to be either kind or harsh. I remember huddling up under my blankets the way I hadn't done since I was eight. I *think* I remember Leah lying down next to me, but she was gone when I woke.

The day crawled by. My manager called once, asking if I was feeling better; I told her no and tried to feel touched when she sounded worried. In the afternoon, Trevor sent me and Leah several e-mails from his office address, carrying multiple links and attachments. I read them without replying. The final message's subject line had degenerated into all-caps begging, and when I saw it was addressed only to me, not Leah, I deleted it unread. I spent some time looking at the photos and videos of Yuri I still had saved on my phone, trying to think what I'd say when whoever eventually went looking for him started to ask questions.

The light from the windows inched across the floor and faded away. I sat in the deepening gloom. Listening. Every hair on my body stretched out, feeling for a chill in the air.

I am coming.

It was mostly dark when Leah finally got home. She waved a sheaf of paper at me as she came in, apparently unsurprised to find me waiting on the couch. "I printed it all out," she said. "Everything Trevor found. What do you think? It makes a lot of sense to me, I have to say."

"I don't know," I said. "If this is something we—we *created*, just out of our minds with that exercise, why don't we have control over it? Why can't we turn it off?"

"Well, we haven't exactly tried, yet." Leah flipped on the lights, came over and sat down beside me, shuffling through the papers. "That Reddit discussion thread, about how to destroy tulpas—"

"Where they all say you just have to stop paying attention to them? How's that been working for you?"

Leah put her hands on her knees and breathed deeply. "The

post near the end," she said, when the color had faded out of her face. "It says one way to actively dissipate a tulpa is to force something into its definition that's essentially a self-contradiction. Like, if you create an imaginary friend, you have to visualize it doing something nobody you call a friend could ever do, like stealing your ex, or . . . or something like that. And then when it can't believe in itself the way it was built to, it falls apart. It literally melts down from the cognitive dissonance."

I snorted. "Yeah, and there are other posts that say the only way to kill a tulpa is to kill whoever created it. Are we buying into that too?"

Leah flushed again. "No! Look, Kris, all I'm saying is that it's worth a shot. I mean, have you got any other ideas?"

Now who's throwing everything back on who? I got up and went to the window, glaring out at the traffic whooshing by outside on Bathurst Street; my legs burned. "We could leave," I said. "Just pick up and get out of here, go as far as we can. See if that makes a difference."

"'We?'" Leah replied.

It was my turn to flush, abrupt and fierce. I opened my mouth to snap *That's not what I meant*, not at all sure what I *had* meant—and coughed out the taken breath in a gasp, heat draining to cold in an instant. "Oh, Christ," I gulped, staring across the street. "Oh, shit—*Leah*." I pointed, amazed to see my hand was shaking. "Do you see that? Tell me you *see* that!"

"See what?" Leah had raced to my side, squinting through our images in the glass. "Hang on—" She dashed back to the door, turned the lights out. Darkness dropped over us. The black figure across the road, a silhouette huddled in the corner of an alley, became sharper, seemed to loom closer up out of the dark. Leah returned to the window; I felt her stiffen. "Oh, shit," she breathed. "Kris, what do we do? What do we *do?*"

Good fucking question. I tried to pull my brain back into one piece. "We could try going out the back door of the main house," I said, voice hoarse. "We'd have to hop the fence, sneak out through the property on the other side, but—"

The figure pushed one hand back awkwardly over its head. Pale hair glinted momentarily in a flicker of the streetlight. And my terror collapsed so completely and quickly into exasperated rage it almost made me puke. "Oh, fuck *me*," I snarled, yanked the window open and stuck my head out. "*Trevor!*" I roared. "*Get your ass over here!*" The black figure jerked; the hat it had been wearing fell off, and Trevor hunched down to grab it as if ducking out of a sniper's line of fire.

"What the hell were you thinking?" I bellowed at him a minute later, on the doorstep of our building. "Were you fucking *trying* to scare us into a heart attack?" Trevor seemed to shrink as I kept yelling; Leah looked like she wanted to say something but couldn't think what. "This is not a fucking game anymore! We don't have time for this kind of stalker bullshit—!"

"I *wasn't*—" Trevor's voice cracked. "I'm not *stalking* you guys, Kris, God! I just—I just want to make sure you're *safe*, okay? Both of you! You're, like, the only people on this planet I give a shit about at all, and if I lost you, I don't—I don't . . ." He trailed off, swallowed liquidly and scrubbed one hand across his face, not looking at me. "You never answered my last e-mail," he finished. "I tried to say it all in there. But you never answered."

Fuck. Of all the times for Leah to be right. I couldn't decide whether to laugh, cry, or scream. "You give a shit about us?" I demanded instead. "Fine. Then fucking *listen* to me and get it through your head: Leah I don't know about, but I am very definitely Gay All Day, and you know that thing about 'if this was the last minute before death would you at least kiss me goodbye?' Hate to say it, man, 'cause you're my friend and I love you *but not like that*—this probably *is* our last minute, and, no. Never. Not ever. Please, just ... go the fuck home and think about it until you get that."

Trevor stared at me for a long time, his eyes wet. "I ... can't," he finally whispered, so quiet I could barely hear him. "I'm scared, Kris."

I sighed, too exhausted for any more anger. "Yeah," I admitted. "Me too. So come in, if you want. But no more of this shit, okay? That's done."

Trevor only nodded, staring at the concrete steps.

I want to say his silence worried me, as we got him set up on the couch to stay the night. I want to say I was thinking about him, at least that much. I want to say I was thinking about anything at all but the sick dread pooling in my stomach and the sounds outside our apartment's front door.

I want to say that all I felt when I went into the bathroom in the morning and saw Trevor hanging from the showerhead, a pair of Leah's hose serving as a noose, was what anybody would feel: shock, horror, anguish, pain. Rage at the pointlessness, the selfishness. Grief like a hole chewing its way through your gut, even before I read his note through streaming eyes: *It took all four of us to make it. Maybe it needs all four of us to keep going. A tulpa dies when its maker dies. Maybe this will break the chain. I'm sorry, Kris. I can't think of any other way.*

I only ever wanted you to be safe.

I was sitting on the cold bathroom floor, note crumpled in my fists, muttering between dry sobs: "Oh, God, Trev, fuck you. *Fuck you*, Trev, God, God ..." when Leah came in, and started to scream. Which finally gave me something else to think about besides the sickening, contemptible truth: In that first moment of comprehension, what I'd felt, more than anything else . . .

. . . was envy.

There wasn't any way to keep the cops out of it this time, though nobody official acted like an asshole. You figure the people who handle this sort of thing learn to tell the fakers from the genuinely traumatized pretty quick most of the time. Not that that's exactly consoling. I remember one bad moment when one of the uniformed officers gave me a narrow look, like something about my no-I-didn't-have-the-slightest-idea-but-he-was-in-therapy answer didn't ring right, but he didn't do anything except give me a card and tell me to call him if I thought of anything else. Leah had cried herself into unconsciousness before anyone had even gotten there, leaving me to handle the clean-up.

After everything was over and everyone was gone, I went into Leah's room and sat at her desk, waiting. For a moment I thought about lying down beside her but couldn't bring myself to do it. The urge didn't last long anyway. Eventually, she woke up and looked at me, and I knew the truth the instant I met her hollow, reddened gaze.

"He's still coming," I said.

Leah only nodded. "He was . . . I recognized the street. It's in Windsor. I grew up there. I could smell the fog . . ." Her voice was raw, a wreck of itself. "This isn't . . . I don't think we made this, Kris. Not completely. Maybe we gave it a shape. But this thing— it's something else. From somewhere else. I think, maybe, it's been looking for a door for a long time." Her gaze dropped to the bedclothes. "And we gave it four of them."

"And wrote it a fucking set of directions," I agreed dully.

Leah frowned, sitting up. "Wait. What if—what if that's it? We wrote its path out for it. Who's to say we can't write its ending the way we want?" Suddenly energized, she swung her legs off the bed and leaned forward to grab my hands. "This whole thing started as a story. Maybe if we want to finish it, we have to *finish* the story."

I stared at her. "Finish it, like . . . how? Just write him going away?"

"Why not?" With what was now almost manic enthusiasm, Leah leapt up, dug her dream journal out of her box, and slammed it down on the desk in front of me. "That's my book, so you'll have to write it, but we can do this right now! Come on, come on . . ." Unable to find words to argue, I let her swivel me around, took the pencil she shoved into my hand as she flipped the journal to a blank page. "Okay. Go for it. Draw the door and write the ending."

"This can't—" But my hand was already moving. Same door as before: rectangle, circle. I closed my eyes and saw shapes move in the blackness. Saw one shape moving slowly, steadily, coming nearer. Leah was muttering in my ear: *The road goes ever on and on, and the traveler must follow, no stops, no destination, no visits; no one waits to welcome him, only the endless road, leaving all other souls behind, untouched, safe in the light, safe in the light, safe in the light as he disappears forever—*

"*Jesus!*" My entire arm suddenly cramped in vicious agony, driving the pencil across the page so hard it tore through the paper and snapped in half. Leah yelped, jumping back. I wrung my hand, feeling blood seeping from my gouged knuckles. "Fuck! Okay, that didn't work."

"No. No, of course it wouldn't, that wasn't an ending, that was just a copout." Leah grabbed the book, flipped to another page and yanked another pen from the desk drawer. "It's a journey, right? Journeys have to *end* somewhere." She sketched a door of her own, this one no more complicated than mine, and paused. "We have to send him somewhere. Somewhere a person couldn't survive; somewhere we *know* nothing could survive." She looked at me expectantly.

I shrugged, at a loss. "Underwater?" I said. "I don't know! Um, underground. Buried." Leah nodded, scribbling furiously. "In space. In the center of the sun ... Wait! No, he wants his door. I don't think we're gonna keep him away from it."

Leah stopped writing and drew a shuddering breath. She never did give up. I'd loved that about her once, before I'd hated how it meant she never let a fight go until she thought *she'd* won it.

"Doors," she said. "That was how it happened with Yuri, too. Maybe—maybe *that's* the key. Not the words. The door." I gaped at her as she turned to one more blank page and, glancing defiantly at me, drew a different rectangle: this one wider than it was tall, with no knob on it or anything else.

"You want to put him inside a wall?" Terror drove through me like freezing water forced down my throat. "No! No, goddammit, Leah, if you do that it's only going to make every wall a door! He'll be able to get in *anywhere!*" I leapt forward and dragged her away from the desk, into the middle of the room, holding her by the shoulders as I cast around wildly. "Oh, Christ, he's close, isn't he? He can fucking hear it in our *heads*! Don't think of him in the walls! Don't!"

Leah shook her head. "No, shit, you're right, you're right ... " She closed her eyes, taking deep breaths, half-determined and half-dismayed. "Not the walls," she muttered, fists clenched. "Not the walls, not the walls, not the—"

She stopped, staring down. I followed her gaze.

Two shadows stretched out in different directions from her feet.

Leah's head snapped up, eyes wide, breath sucking in. "Oh, shit, *Kri*—" was all she got out, before two massive arms made of something that looked like molten tar exploded out of the floor, wrapped around her and jerked her back down into it. Under. Through. *Away.*

So that was three days ago. I've been working on this ever since, on Leah's laptop.

I told my boss I wasn't coming back to work, after which I unplugged Leah's landline and turned off both her phone and mine. There was a banging on the door yesterday that sounded like a cop's knock, but I just stopped moving and didn't say anything. After a while it stopped. I haven't eaten much or slept much. Strangely, when I do sleep, I don't dream.

And now you know why you shouldn't ever have started reading, whoever's reading this. Because he gets stronger the closer he gets. If you know about him, he knows about you. The only thing I can think of is that if enough people learn about him, he'll be—I don't know, maybe dispersed somehow. Like a drop of ink disappearing in a lake. I want to believe that, because I don't have anything left to think about the alternative.

And maybe if all I do is give him more people to . . . to take, he'll be grateful enough that whatever he does with me, whenever he *does* come for me, maybe I'll at least end up where Leah is. Wherever she went. Wherever Yuri went. I want to hope maybe somehow Trevor will be there, too, but I don't know how reasonable that is—

Reasonable. Jesus Christ. I just wrote the word *reasonable.*

Maybe I should have tried harder to make this story unreadable, unbelievable. Forgettable. But that's the trick about forgetting: you can't ever really choose to do it. You can only wait and hope it happens. Sit in an empty apartment, breathing as quietly as you can. You can try to unfocus your eyes. Try not to read. Try not to recognize words. Try not to put them together.

Try not to think of water.

Try not to think of darkness.

Try not to think of the inside of your wall.

Try not to think of the inside of the sun.

Try not to think of the inside of your own body. Of the inside of your own head.

Try not to think of anything.

Try to think of nothing.

Venio: A Commentary

ONE OF THE REASONS GEMMA FILES IS SUCH A good horror writer—and not only a masterful fantasist—is because she fearlessly goes after her reader's mind, sadistically even. "Venio" is just such a story, where the reader is warned right from the opening line to "watch out." But this warning is merely a lure: the story seeks to inhabit us in a way that will haunt us both during the reading experience and forever after.

"Venio" is framed as a memory of a writer, regretting a creativity game or writing exercise, that somehow conjures a pursuit by a seemingly inescapable supernatural entity that generates a sense of unease as haunting as the 2014 horror film, *It Follows*. But it's not just a creepy piece of first person narrative rife with moments of second-person direct address. It literally makes use of "you" (the addressed second person, the reader), trapping you in its unforgettable conclusion.

Unforgettable, indeed.

As is made plain in the story's final lines—again, like the opening frame of the narrative, structured as warnings to "try not to think" of anything—the reader is a character, too. In other words, "Venio" is not just a clever horror story, but an embodiment of what literary critic Frederic Jameson termed the "prison-house of language." That is, the structure of story is a kind of trap, where the system of signs that make up a word, sentence, or story are a conceit where "meaning" only means itself. The final line—"try to think of nothing"—is the ultimate of endings, an ironic twist on absence and what it means to die, insofar as language and storytelling is concerned.

This story stalks you. Try not to think about it too much. Else . . .

—Michael Arnzen, PhD

Sown from Salt

They made a desert there, and called it peace.

—Tacitus.

REESE WOKE AFTER DAWN, DEW-STIFF, WITH difficulty; so much blood had dried all over his face, while he slept, that his eyelashes were now almost too sticky to peel open. The hard Arizona sun pressed down on him. Aside from the song of flies, no other living creature seemed anywhere near.

Though there did not seem to be much to bother rousing himself for, he sat up moments later nonetheless, and nearly threw up. A terribly familiar pain monopolized the center of his chest, folding him up around itself like a half-screwed winch. Had he not known better, he might have thought the bullet in him still, lodged deep—a truly unlovely thing, harbinger of delirium and death. Yet neither of those was to be his portion anymore, as he was well aware.

There was a dead body laying almost next to him, one of several such—leftovers from the latest trip to yet another town, fresh and not-so alike, scattered where they fell after judgement— but he ignored it; dead bodies were everywhere. This world was a butcher-shop at the best of times. He'd've been far more surprised not to find one, there or elsewhere, on top of the earth or under it.

Eventually, he made his feet and stood there swaying, squinting upward. He felt for his watch, popped it open, checked the time and reckoned which direction might be north accordingly: left a bit, where that dry ravine-mouth hid the horizon, aided by scrubby bushes. Some hours hard walking to anything resembling civilization, probably, which alone argued for getting going. Yet he stood there a moment more, unsteady, wishing with all his considerable might that he could simply lie back down and sleep, this time without fear of waking.

His mouth already too dry for spit, he drew a cambric handkerchief from one pocket and used it, fastidiously, to scrub his sticky lashes clean. His eyes burned.

Grimly, he staggered forward.

Never fully alone, even in this emptiest of places; as the sun moved overhead, shimmering mirages lit the corners of his eyes; Reese seemed to hear distant laughter, footsteps behind and whinnying horses ahead, even brief snatches of song—a plaintive hill-holler tune from old Missouri, Mother of Outlaws, sung in the most easily recognizable of light baritones:

I wish I wish . . . my baby was born . . . and sittin' on . . . his Daddy's knee . . . and me, poor gal, was dead and gone . . . and the green grass growin' over me . . .

. . . at which point he fell, taking almost a whole half-hour to rise again. Lay curled 'round his pain once more, cracked lips fresh-split, and sang the chorus back in a bare whisper all the while, not even one-quarter so effortlessly pretty:

" . . . but that's not now, nor never will be . . . 'til the sweet apple grows . . . on the sour apple tree . . . "

He had a man kept in his mind to go with that voice, same as always; last thing he'd seen before that dark crack between then and now first gaped wide, not to mention the only thing he'd remembered consistently since. Those mocking eyes finding his, full-on, right before obscene pain broke his world apart in a spurt of gun-smoke. They had looked at each other, and then he had been looking at the ground, and then he had been looking at nothing. And then—

—and then, after . . . much later . . . he had woken up once more, dew-stiff and cold on the hard desert ground, his heart apparently having been replaced by an open wound. With someone else's blood dried to a sticky mask all over his stupidly dumbfounded face.

He rose back up, walked on, 'til the sun met the horizon. 'Til everything went gold, then red, then black.

The next town he crossed over into—sometime after sunset, under a mean sprinkling of star—was so small he somehow knew (as he always did, these days) it only had one whore left working, and her kept so indifferently busy, she often had to take in piecework to make ends meet. They'd had setbacks, obviously, almost since foundation; a virtual parade of ill-luck with no apparent cause (or cure), forever conspiring to rob the place of reason for being. Hope of mining had first inspired settlers to congregate there, 'til the claims dried up. They'd then switched to raising livestock—sheep, pigs, cattle, horses—'til various sicknesses forced those not bankrupted outright to cultivate a host of crops, all of which similarly came to nothing. Now there was intermittent talk of the Railroad, which might (or might not) be drifting toward their territory.

Jesus, too, had persisted strongly throughout all of the above—camp-meetings, revivals, the occasional church of some Revelation or other always raising itself up and flourishing briefly before falling away again to ruin—though that in itself had never, as yet, proved much of a draw for attracting new citizenry.

He passed the gutted shell of one such project on the town's west-most outskirt. Someone had propped a sign against its door-lintel, done unpunctuated, in shaky red letters of varying size: *MaNy cry in Truble & Are not hEard But to there SalvatioN.*

"Saint Augustine," he said, out loud, recognizing the words as ones his former "friend" had once quoted him, in time of particular moral quandary—for the man in question did love to read, and loved even better to let others know just how well-read he was.

That struggle with his own impulses—let alone their shared actions—had been a passing one, he now recalled; easily overturned by sentiment, if not by argument. As ever.

Because: *We've all done things we regret, I expect*, his "friend" had allowed, though both of 'em knew full well the other probably didn't think he had. To which he'd paused and considered, trying his level best to summon even one instance in which he'd genuinely questioned himself. Replying, finally—

I do wish I hadn't stayed my hand, at Lincoln.

His "friend" smiled at that, narrowly: *Didn't much, from what I hear.*

Not too much, no. But whenever I did, I wish I hadn't.

And did he feel differently, now? Could he even tell *how* he felt, if—indeed—he felt anything, at all?

But here were the lights of what passed for a main street, at last: Open doorways, noise and music, faces peering out to greet him as he limped toward them in his dusty motley, his sticky crimson finery. He aimed to at least reach that storefront which claimed a doctor resided within before he pitched over, face-forward, to wait for them to decide what best to do with him . . .

and this he was indeed able to achieve, before darkness reclaimed him. The never-quite-broken-off song rising undimmed in his ears, like blood, like tide:

I wish I wish . . . my love had died . . .
And set his spirit roaming free . . .
So we might meet where ravens fly
And never longer parted be . . .

(But that's not now, nor never will be)

"Mister. Mister, do you know where you are?"

A gruffer voice, from some farther distance off:

"'Course he don't, Doc—don't even know his own name, I bet. How long you think he's been walkin'?"

The doc sighed. "Couldn't rightly say, not without I question him directly. Help me shift him up on that table, will you?"

This last was followed by a vertiginous rush and roll of movement, balanced ineptly with a hand or two on every slack limb before he came crashing down again, his skull connecting table-top-ward with a sick little crack. And: "Not so hard!" The doc cried, fussily. "You'll tear his scalp open, start him back to bleedin'—"

Then came the gruff voice once more, chiming back in— someone in authority: Sheriff, Mayor? Or both? Saying:

"You sure that's all *his* blood, Doc? 'Cause he don't look too 'sanguinated to me, from where *I* sit."

He didn't have to open his eyes to "see" the doc's mouth crimp at that, unbelieving. "Well, I suppose I don't quite take your meaning, Mister Marten. For pity's sake, whose else would it likely to *be*?"

"That's the question, all right," Marten murmured.

When he did open his eyes, some hours later, they came apart smoothly; someone had finally run a hot cloth over his face, paying special attention to all those varying nooks and crannies where the blood had collected most deeply.

He got up, still moving slowly—didn't seem to move any other way, these days. He remembered how his pulse had once run so hot, his every movement a fever, resting heartbeat faster than a grouse across level ground. In the pier-glass above the wash-basin, he saw his own pale visage blink back at him: Bushwhacker hair to below his shoulders, meticulously groomed in anticipation of whenever the South might rise again, plus a narrow blond beard and luxuriant moustachios, a pistoleer Musketeer; sand-light eyes under similarly bleached lashes, almost yellow from some angles.

And: *Why, Sergeant,* he thought, *I never looked to see* you *here, down amongst the dead men and the drifting trash. Not without your dear companion to spur you along in any necessary endeavors, at any rate.*

Oh, but it was bitter, too, no matter how he might try to smile at it; the pain inside him felt abruptly greater than before, not that it ever grew small. So hollow with grief and hate and longing that it fair came off of him in waves, the way heat boils up from the veiny crust of some fallow field at noon. In that one dreadful moment he at last knew himself little more than a husk set endlessly roaming this world, always in search of one who fled from him (as youth flees from youth, or shadow flees from light), and might well have wept at such terrible understanding, had the desert not long since rendered him incapable.

But now there was a knocking at the door, impatient for entry; he stood there stock-still, unable to hide his true nature anymore. Spotting his guns slung over a chair by the bed-stead even as they kicked through, and knowing himself far too slow to reach them before *they* broke through their initial shock at seeing him laid thus bare, jumping forward all at once to take him down in a single sprawling pile.

Face-on, Sheriff Marten proved as bluff and craggy a Union bastard as any Reese'd ever plugged through the brain-pan, or anywhere else. Marten held up a broadsheet from which the same face he'd seen mirrored upstairs stared, wall-eyed; next to it his "friend" quirked just the slightest of smiles, as though thinking it a fine irony that they meet again this way.

"Your name Sartain Reese, same's it says here?" Marten asked.

"Sartain Stannard Reese, yes."

"Folks call you 'One-Shot'?"

"They do."

Marten's deputy, a clean-browed young man whose eyes were masked by little round-lensed spectacles, put in, at that: "You really at Lincoln, Reese?"

"When I was fifteen, yes."

"And I guess you was at Bewelcome, too," Marten said. "With Bart Haugh."

" . . . yes."

"Uh huh. So where's that sumbitch now?"

Reese glanced down, head hung low, ridiculous hair falling between them like a shield; replied, carefully—fighting hard to keep any further tremor from his already-shaky voice, which thankfully might be put down to him having been punched in both throat and belly during their earlier tussle—

"Don't rightly know. We had a fallin' out."

"What happened?"

At this Reese looked up again, grinning against the pain, and tapped his chest one time above the breast-bone, neat and clean and hard, like knocking on a coffin's lid. Saying:

"Well, as to that . . . he shot me, Sheriff, just about here. You see it, where I'm pointin'? Right through my goddamned heart."

Marten stared him straight in the eye, unimpressed by what he maybe took for mere rhetoric. "So how're you alive then, Mister Reese?"

Reese nodded, slightly. "How am I?" He repeated, without much emphasis. Having already asked himself that same question on many an occasion by now, and never yet received any satisfactory answer.

They beat on him some more for a while, after, before slinging him into a cell to wait on some judge they'd have to order from two towns over. The deputy (Jenkins, his name proved to be) sat there checking Reese's guns in front of him, stroking their chased silver hilts admiringly and sighting down their long barrels at nothing in particular, before locking them safely away with the rest of the sheriff's armaments.

"Wouldn't do that, I was you," Reese told him, carefully maneuvering one of his looser teeth around in its socket with his tongue-tip.

Jenkins frowned. "Why not?"

"'Cause unless you're planning on selling 'em, you probably don't want what comes along with 'em. They was at Lincoln too, after all."

Jenkins gave him a long, cool look. "I heard some things, about you and Haugh."

"Did you, now." A pause. "Well, since I think I know what, I don't suppose it'll do either of us much good to discuss it any further. Still—would you say I merited hangin' less or more, I wonder, you happened to find out they was true?"

"There's some would say more," Jenkins allowed, flushing slightly. "But I ain't with 'em on that one, necessarily."

"Kind of you. I *do* merit it, though, sure enough—for Bewelcome, and elsewhere. Make no mistake about that."

That shut Jenkins up, at least for a little bit; must've been something he saw reflected in Reese's eyes, under the lantern's uncertain light. They maintained silence together, oddly companionable, until he finally had to ask—

"Whose blood was that you had on you, Reese?"

"Oh, somebody from 'round here's, I expect. Didn't you recognize it?" A pause. "Listen, Jenkins—you and yours seem good people, on the whole, from what I've seen. But there's always a reason I run across places, and you *have* been unlucky, so might be that's 'cause there's other people here, ones that's *just like me*."

Jenkins, paling: "I'd know, if there was."

Reese really did have to laugh then, torn mouth bleeding just a bit as he did, streaking his smile like rouge. "Would you? How, exactly, saving the Word of God? Men lie, Jenkins, even when they *don't* have something to hide—so how much more you think they're prepared to do to cover true sin up, 'specially if they don't want to have to keep on runnin' from its consequences?"

Which brought silence again, for a spell. Reese drank it in, leaned his head back against the cell wall, and waited.

As it soon turned out, the rest of the townsfolk didn't plan on putting anything off for simple lack of a judge. Instead, they came for Reese at midnight, with guns and torches; shouted Marten and Jenkins down, then hustled him back down Cow-track Avenue and hung him from a tree outside that same burnt church he'd passed on his way into town. They also proved inexpert enough at this particular form of semi-judicial murder that his neck failed to break on the drop, which meant he dangled there a while—tongue out and blackening, face a-swell, some awful noise issuing forth from his throat like a half-swallowed rattlesnake—before Jenkins finally lunged forward and hauled at both his legs together 'til the crack of bone rang out at last.

This last mercy loosed a flood of piss that ran down Reese's fine trousers to foul them from the crotch down, soiling dirt and deputy alike; as he thrashed, strangling, his gay shirt flew open in front, revealing to all and sundry the black miracle of his wound . . . that awful fleshly Advent Calendar with only one day left celebrated, laid open like a little bone window so everyone in town could see the cold pink meat framed underneath its ragged hole, unbroken yet unbeating.

He heard more than one woman or close-hugged child shriek out in terror at the sight, while many more than one man blasphemed in gutter-language he recognized from Lincoln, Dodge City, Bewelcome itself. But then the penultimate buzz was in his ears, drowning out even that damn betraying song, at long long last:

The owl the owl . . . is a lonesome bird . . .
It chills my heart with dread and terror . . .
That's someone's blood there on its wing,
That's someone's blood there on its feather . . .

Then Reese was not,
nor never would be,
strung to rot like fruit
from a gallows-tree.

But it wasn't the end, of course; never was. Not since he'd woken that first morning with blood in his eyes, his mouth, his hair—with an open wound where his shot-through heart should be, and Bart Haugh's faithless name still curdled on his lips.

By dawn on the third day he was deep in unhallowed ground, sand and stones piled haphazardly atop to ward off coyotes. But the morning opened dark above his grave, only to grow steadily darker, a storm lowering constantly overhead yet never breaking fully into much-needed rainfall, while ball- and sheet-lightning chased each other up and down the sullen, swollen sky.

And just after sunset, once more, was when Reese came limping into town again, up the main street to Marten's office, covered in the same dirt and piss they'd buried him wearing. His tongue black-tinged yet in a still-torn mouth, when he opened it to wish Sheriff Marten and Deputy Jenkins alike a raspy—

"Good even, gentlemen."

Marten gaped. "Sweet King Christ Jesus, 'One-Shot' Reese."

"That'd be a 'no' to the first, 'yes' to the second," Reese replied, with all the bleak coolness of his condition. Adding, to Jenkins: "Now, I'd much appreciate havin' my guns back, Deputy, if you don't mind; they were a gift, you see. And the plain truth is, I'm sentimental about such things."

Jenkins nodded a tad at this, as though he quite took Reese's point—but Marten drew his own sidearm instead, aiming it straight at Reese's midsection. Blustering: "*You* can just go right on back to Hell and *stay* there, this time, you damned murderin' secesh—"

Reese shook his head, dusty gold hair flapping a bit with the gathering wind. "I believe there's some following behind me may want a few words with you, Sheriff, on that very same subject."

He said it gently, though—perhaps too much so. For under cover of that howl-din which suddenly rose up all around them, a great chorus of disembodied plaint knit to a hundred skittering shadows, Reese's warning seemed almost entirely lost on Marten, whose eyes grew wide and crazed. Even as Jenkins turned to inquire if he was all right, the sheriff found himself abruptly surrounded by nothing and borne away in some phantom twister of screams, kicking and yelling, bound for whatever black country Reese had already left behind.

Now it was Jenkins' turn to freeze, face slack and wondering. For all over the rest of town, similar harsh magic was being worked: A new-made widow far too infatuate with her state over here, a rival whose dispute had been settled through apparent chance over there; one veteran who boasted, another who did not; those with unsupported claims to their pasts, as well as those who never spoke of what had brought them there at all. Interestingly, almost none of Reese's own lynch-gang were to be counted amongst the judged—save for one or two Jenkins knew had once delivered other, similarly rough, instances of frontier "justice."

Reese—who had seen this same drama played out many times previously, in many different places—ignored it all, strolling past Jenkins into the sheriff's vacant office, where he broke the weapons cabinet's lock with Marten's empty desk-chair. As he walked back out, adjusting his holsters down low on his hips, he found Jenkins there to meet him... and paused, courteously, barely flinching, to let the deputy bury a few slugs in his gut; the very least he could offer, as recompense for the night's awfulness. Nothing poured from the wounds except for a few slack streams of sand and reddish dust, admixed.

Reese peered at Jenkins, frozen once more, some vague semblance of sympathy in his yellow eyes. "Feel better?" he asked.

Jenkins swallowed. "Why him? Why not me?"

"Well, he had blood on him too, I expect. You don't. Not yet, anyhow." Turning away: "Better look to keep it that way in future, don't you think?"

He left Jenkins standing there—probably the town's best choice for new sheriff, now—and made off, without much haste, down that muddy cart-route which might never quite pass for a true main thoroughfare, while dark tides of vengeance eddied back and forth all about him, leaving few but him (their harbinger, their slave) untouched. Musing as he did on how Bart Haugh, always over-proud of his Eastern university learning, had once read from *Bullfinch's Mythology* the tale of King Cadmus, who killed the dragon guarding the river outside Thebes-to-be, knocked out all its teeth, and sowed 'em in the nearby fields . . . like seed, like salt. Then stood there astounded when men came up instead of crops, all over armor, and did what men in armor do best . . .

Amusing once, now the story was only bitter true: He knew himself a walking dragon's tooth, sent to lie in other folks' earth a while, and see what might rise up along with him, afterward. And yet, even supposing some variety of judgement (divine, or otherwise) drove what he did, he could never count what he brought along with him as vengeance, not even for whatever the people there might wreak on him beforehand; as he'd told Jenkins, *that* was only what he deserved. If he were to be hung in every town from here to Missouri, it still might not be enough to wash him clean of everything he'd done.

On reaching the western-most border of town, Reese paused again, craning his neck to the sky. And cried out, to no one in particular—

"There. Am I done yet? Can I *stop*?"

Silence, only; the lightning's flash, clouds a-boil like lava. Reese felt it twist in him, knife-like, 'til he could not restrain his next demand, torn cold and bloody from the dry hole where his perforated heart should keep time still, unbreached. Screaming up at those hidden, condemning stars, 'til his throat fair cracked:

"Look, just—where in the hell *is* he, goddamnit? So I know which way to go, at least! You want me to keep on working Your will much longer, You surely need to *tell* me, *right damn now*—"

But: Nothing replied, as he'd come to expect, save for the thunder, which cracked the vault above him open, wide, to loose the promised torrent. A scarlet, sticky rain, warm and salt, which fell only on him, soaking him from tip to toe with the leavings of his own sin. Covering him completely, erasing all he was, or might have been.

An answer, of sorts—long-expected, bitter in his torn mouth, on his blackened tongue. So Sartain Stannard Reese bowed his proud Bushwhacker head to the wind of comeuppance, prepared to walk until he fell. Knowing that by the time the sun rose he would wake yet again, dew-stiff and cold, crusted all over with blood not his own. That he would seek his "friend"-turned-enemy Bart Haugh eternally and never find him, for vengeance . . . once that most satisfactory of all commodities . . . was no longer his to administer.

Not now. Nor never.

He set his raw feet to the desert's hard road, therefore, that same song dinning ceaseless in his ears. And let darkness take him, praying that this time—*this* time, of innumerable other occasions—

—it would not be so unkind as to even play at letting him go, once more.

SOWN FROM SALT: A COMMENTARY

"SOWN FROM SALT" SHOWS FILES'S TALENT FOR writing horror stories set in the Old West. Her description of everything from grizzly gunslingers to the dry desert sand feels so uncannily accurate to the period, and she does a masterful job with diction and point of view here, telling a tall tale of frontier justice that is slightly reminiscent of *High Plains Drifter* (1973), but harkens even further back into ancient mythology, bringing in dragons and legendary song, and more surprises I won't give away here. This story has a lesson to depart, surely, regarding justice and remaining ever-vigilant against evil, but it is also about eternal suffering, punishment, and identity. Who is the main character, Reese, really? *Why* is Reese what he is, and damned too, to begin with? There are no simple answers, save for the notion that "One-Shot Reese" is a metaphor for us all on some level. We walk the earth. We hope for an end that makes sense, but it is beyond our control.

—Michael Arnzen, PhD

GUISING

WHEN I WAS A KID, OUT IN THE WOODS ON THE
Dourvale Shore, I saw faces in the bushes, sometimes: wizened like
nuts, smooth like peeled birch, smiling, snarling, but always with
holes—small or large, dark or empty—where you'd expect their
eyes to be. Sometimes, at night, I saw wavery little versions of those
faces looking out of my bedroom walls, from the spaces in the
pattern of the wallpaper.

You probably think I'm speaking metaphorically. Everyone
else did, for years—said it was just hypnagogic imagery, a kind of
waking dream, a manifestation of the trauma going on around me.
And after getting tired of attempting to persuade them otherwise,
I eventually managed to kind of convince myself they were right.

But I really wasn't speaking metaphorically then, and I'm sure
not doing it now.

I remember trying to draw the face I saw most, then having
that drawing taken away from me by my grandmother, who
burned it in her iron-bellied kitchen stove. I remember she and my
dad arguing about it, later on, when they thought I couldn't hear.

This was just after my parents broke up, when Dad took us
home to Overdeere, to stay with his mother until he got a job
that'd support us. He'd been a late baby, and as a result, my
grandmother was the single oldest person I'd ever seen. Her heavy
braid of hair was the dull brownish-yellow of nicotine stains,
matching the DuMaurier cigarettes she was always chain-smoking,
her hands wrinkly-soft and peppered with age-spots. She kept her

teeth in a jar and her own "eyes" in a case—they were contact lenses, really, but that didn't stop my dad from telling me, when I asked once where Grandma was: "Oh, she's upstairs, sweetie, taking her eyes out."

"I'll be out of here by Christmas," Dad told her, to which she simply sniffed.

"You'd better be," she replied.

Dad and Mom just didn't get along anymore, was how he'd eventually explained it, and I'd nodded as though I agreed—though, looking back, I found I couldn't really remember when they had. They were different people, to say the least; she came "from town," which in this case was Barrie, and had hoity ideas about what constituted decent living standards. Dad, on the other hand, was a Lake of the North boy, born and bred—managed to bull his way through a Forestry degree, but not quite to find a place in his preferred area. She'd stood there with a disapproving look on her face, watching him slip down into a Rona Gardening job ("You'd be a glorified florist, Kieran!") which eventually became unbearable, after which he got his trucker's license and began to do long-haul, gone three weeks out of every four. Her own stuff she could do from home, at night—she'd majored in Computer Tech, with a Design minor, which kept her busy building other people's websites. But it wasn't enough.

I don't blame her, I guess—not now, anyways. But I did then.

Most days, in fact, I can barely remember her face, aside from that one photo the papers found, reduced to newsprint or LCD pixels. All I have left of her is her scent, a celebrity perfume they don't make anymore, and the memory that the day she finally took off, she was wearing her favourite set of green ribbons trimmed with silver foil in her long, dark hair. Just gone, out the door and down the road in a cab to meet the boyfriend we'd never known she had. And the next day, Dad's car pulled out of our former driveway in the exact opposite direction, with me riding shotgun and everything we had in the back.

A week later, we were setting up in my grandmother's spare room, where the air stung with dust and the furniture hadn't been updated since 1973. Its single window looked straight out into the top sections of a British-style boundary-setting hedgerow whose roots her own grandfather supposedly laid, but which had been left to grow wild since the Korean War. Before that, however, the old man had done his work well—the fruit of his labors grew ten feet high and three feet deep, forming a close-knit lattice of stick-bone bars in winter, a mulch-fed mini-forest every other time of year. What light seeped through was green, and when you stood right next to it, your hands and face turned pallid, bruisy, veins gone suddenly delicate under leaf-thin skin. The shadows it cast made you look as though your blood had turned to chlorophyll.

"Best to stay out of the woods, kiddo," Dad told me, that first day. "It's an obstacle course, back there—deadfalls everywhere. A kid I knew growing up fell down a crevasse once, broke his leg, didn't get found for almost a week. Never was right in the head, after that."

"Don't forget the Hell Holes," my grandmother called, from the kitchen.

"Yeah, that's right." To me: "There's Hell Holes, too—sudden falls, straight down, nobody even knows how deep. The limestone forms bubbles, just gives way underfoot."

"It's because of the swamps. That's where the sulphur gas comes from, too."

"Hydrogen sulfide, Mom. It just smells like sulphur."

"Same difference! That stuff'll knock you out, and it catches on fire, you aren't careful. So no mucking 'round with matches!"

"She's not gonna do that, Mom. You're not gonna do that, honey, are you?"

"No, Dad," I lied.

— ✳ —

It was hard to find a way under the hedge, but I finally managed it. I had to dig around at the bottom, where the stakes holding the ethers in place had started to break down, 'til I found a place so damaged by underground digging, frost and blight that a pathway large enough to crawl through had opened up. It was narrower than me, but I wriggled through, like a worm—emerged on the other side covered in juice-stains and dirt, with cobwebs in my hair and bugs down the neck of my sweater. When I slid it off to scrub my face, a grasshopper fell out, still kicking.

Beyond, the woods began in progress, with no clear line of demarcation. You just looked up, and there they were; there *you* were, more to the point. Where the trees came in so close they shut out the sky, ferns grew so deep you couldn't see where to step, and every weed you brushed past left part of itself behind— clinging, scratching, stinging. The only way out was up, through the underbrush, the terrain getting steeper until weeds gave way to moss and the hill beneath emerged: a massive, pinky-gray blister of granite scored with hand-deep gouges where fresh acorns collected, cushioned on a rotten mush of old ones.

When I got up high enough, the rock flattened out, forming a little shelf, maybe three feet by six. And on that shelf I found an equally tiny camp-table center-set, haphazardly nailed together from wood, stripped gray by weather. The hill went up behind it, so slant it formed a sort of seat, so I plumped myself down and looked at the tabletop, where a word had been carved, in strangely beautiful script: SARACEN.

"That's my cousin's name," a voice said, from behind me.

Another little girl had come up, so silently I'd never heard her. She was literally leaning out of the brush above, hanging in over my shoulder, so close I couldn't even jump; denied room to react, my heart just gave a little knock, and I looked at her, swallowing.

"Oh?" I managed, finally. "Uh ... that's cool. I never heard of a guy named Sara ... "

She corrected me: "Sara*cen,* his name is. They're folk from away, unbelievers in Turkish climes, on the other side of the world. My mother says his mother liked the sound of it, when she was carrying." She peered down at the carving with interest. "Must be he played here too, once, though I can barely credit it."

"They live nearby, your family?"

"All around. We're many, hereabouts."

"We just moved here. Well, Dad and me."

"Aye, I ken. You're Jess Nuttall's boy's girl."

"My name's Nuala. What's yours?"

"They call me Leaf."

She had a high, hoarse voice, not much wind to it, and rough, though that might have been the rhythm of her speech. I was too young to know her accent—it all just seemed strange to me, foreign somehow, with no clear idea beyond that. Years later, it occurred to me that she sounded as though she'd learned English from someone with a thick Scots burr, but spoke it with most of a North Ontarian honk, aside from certain differences of pronunciation.

"How old are you?" I asked. "I'm nine."

She struck a theatrical pose and told me, deadpan: "Oh, I am old, old. I have seen five forests come and go, but never before have I seen beer brewed in an eggshell."

I goggled at her. "You're kidding, right?" And she laughed, high and sweet, a child's laugh like any other, save how I immediately wanted to hear it again.

"Cert," she said. "I'm ... kidding, only. I have nine years as well, myself."

Looking back, I can see that she said the word "kidding" as

though she'd never heard it before, but liked it. It made her grin, wide, which in turn showed how charmingly gappy her teeth all were, not to mention larger than you'd expect given her size. So much so that when she put her jaws back together, I swear I saw her bottom canines slightly dent her upper lip.

"Do you guise?" she asked, a moment later. Then explained, spurred by my obvious bafflement: "Put on a face, I mean—make masks, pretend."

"Like . . . play dress-up, is that it? Or like for Hallowe'en?"

"Aye, that. All Hallows. Samhain Night."

"Well, sure, I guess. Don't you?"

"Aye, ever. We call it the glamour."

"*The* glamour?"

"So I said."

Leaf and I played for what didn't seem like hours, but when I realized the sun was going down, I started back. "You could come for dinner," I offered, not actually knowing if that would be okay with my grandmother or not. But she just shook her shaggy head, solemnly.

"I'm wanted home," she said. "And besides . . . no, better not."

"You can come anytime," I said. "Tomorrow, maybe."

"Or you, up here."

"I'm starting school soon. Will I see you there?"

"Not too like."

" . . . tomorrow, then. Here."

She laughed again. "Aye," she said. "If I don't see you, first."

You're wondering why I'm telling you all this, no doubt. Like *what's the damn point, Nuala?* And then you maybe remember what I let slip about my mother, back there—what I grazed over, more like, without explanation—and think, annoyed: *More about that,* that's *what I'd like to know.* Not all this backwoods *Stand By Me* crap—"it was the best of summers, it was the worst of summers . . ." I mean, Jesus.

Well, at the time, for me, my mother had already disappeared. None of us would know anything more until six months later, when two nice officers from the Ontario Provincial Police came asking whether or not we'd had contact with her since a month previously. We were as surprised as anybody else to discover she'd apparently left that boyfriend of hers the same way she'd left us, except far more precipitately: without warning, in the middle of the night, leaving all of her stuff behind. None of which kept the OPP from making him their primary suspect; he had a record, after all, though most of it was for minor drug charges and public intoxication.

A year after that, some hikers exploring the fens around Chaste found her purse nestled high in a tree. Inside was her wallet, most of her hair and a few of her teeth, fresh enough to get DNA from the pulp and roots. My mother's boyfriend was arrested, protesting vociferously. The Crown argued that he probably threw her down a Hell Hole, of which there are several in Chaste's vicinity, though why he didn't do the same with her purse was never explored. That they found a thriving grow-op inside his garage probably didn't help.

He's been in jail for over ten years now, up at the Kingston Pen. I was asked to make a victim's statement at his first parole hearing, but I told them it would upset me too much, which they accepted. I was later informed that he did not, in fact, make parole, because he'd been caught multiple times holding drugs for other inmates.

These are the facts. The truth, so far as I've since been able to figure it, is rather more slippery, and difficult to prove—as it often is. But here, in particular . . .

Much like beer brewed in eggshells, what came next is definitely odd enough to merit comment, no matter *how* old you might be.

At school I soon fell in with a little group of kids my age. Still, I always found a reason to sneak off and meet up with Leaf, at least a couple days a week. She showed me paths I could never find again on my own, taking us all around the area: to the Lake, the dumps out back of the Sidderstane cannery, even that overgrown ghost-village by the Dourvale Shore my new friends talked about in whispers. One afternoon in October, we sat together inside a salt-box house whose interior had fallen to ruin, leaving only the outermost portions: four windowless walls, crooked and rickety, held together mainly with vines. Two trees grew up through the middle, where the floor used to be, and their branches made a sort of roof.

"And where's she now?" Leaf asked.

"Don't know," I replied. Then added, quickly, as though to convince myself: "Don't much care, either. She never bothered to call since we got here, never even bothered to write . . . I mean, not like she doesn't know where we *are*. She just doesn't give a heck, so screw her."

Leaf nodded. "Mothers shouldn't leave," she said. "It's not right."

I laughed, bitter. "I'm okay without one, I guess," I said. "So, what about *your* mom? She nice?"

"Oh, I love her dearly. Her, my brothers and sisters, our cousins . . ."

"No dad?"

"Somewhere," she said. "We don't make ourselves, aye? But

he's no part of us, really." Since I didn't know what to say to that, we sat a few more minutes in silence, watching the trees move overhead—comfortable, somehow, even in our discomfort. I could hear her breathing, a faint, sighing song, same as the wind which scattered dead leaves at our feet.

"I'd help with your sorrows, Nuala, if I could," Leaf told me, eventually, putting her cold little hand on mine, with an odd gentleness; I remember how overlong her nails were, black at the broken tips, and that they scratched just a bit, for all her restraint. Looking up at me under the shaggy fringe of her hair, her eyes ever-so-slightly a-gleam, and asking: "You know so, don't you? For you're my friend, my only."

"I know, Leaf."

"Though you have friends elsewhere, now, I hear."

"What, Grace and Milton, Heather? They're just kids in my class, like—somebody to eat lunch with, or hang at recess. *You're* my *best* friend."

"And you, for me, always." She nodded at the sky, like she saw something floating up there, coming closer. "Will be All Hallows soon. Do you think to guise that night, and walk out begging?"

"Um, not so much. I mean, there's that thing at school, the costume party. But we're all a little old for trick or treat, right?"

Her face fell. "I'd hoped you would," she said, at last. "For my family celebrates that night, and I'd have you meet them, if I may. 'Tis a great rout, always."

"Well..." And now I felt bad. "Where do they have it, usually?"

"Oh, hereabouts. The Shore's ours, to do with as we please." She gave me a shy glance. "I could come meet you, the night of, at your school. Bring you here."

I hesitated. "You do that, the guys'll want to come along too."

"Then let them. All will have safe passage, so long as I'm near."

In the trees, a bird sang; the sun was sinking, colors changing. The wind blew a little colder, and I shivered, even in my jacket.

"Sure," I said, finally. "That'd be good."

Dad was out on a run, Hallowe'en week; he'd gotten his passport updated the month before, so it probably involved crossing the border. Which left my grandmother and me rattling around together, me working on my costume, her doing the stuff she usually did.

"What do you know about fairies, Nuala?" she asked me, the night before: Devil's Night, Mischief Night, when all the older kids were supposedly out egging houses and TP-ing trees. Then continued, not waiting for an answer: "In the old days, my folks used to say Hallowe'en was when they let the ghosts of the damned out of Hell, and that's why we dressed up—so they wouldn't know who we were, if they met us out after dark. You go back further still, though, it wasn't ghosts they meant at all, but the *Daoine Sidhe*, the good folk. Them under the hill."

"What hill, Grandma?"

"Any hill, I guess. But 'round here, they mostly meant Druir Hill, on the Dourvale Shore; don't suppose you go anyplace near there, do you, when you crawl out under the hedge?" At that I looked up, shocked, which made her give a grim little smile. "Oh yes, my girl, I know all about that—think you were the first ever got that same notion? Think again."

"*You* did?"

"Many a time. Up the hill, past that table . . . there was a boy I'd meet there, sometimes, came right out of the woods. Mrs. Sidderstane's son, from up at the big house, who wrote his name on the table-top with his knife."

Saracen, I thought. *Unbeliever, from away.*

"Oh, and he was handsome, too, with his blue eyes, though there was something about the way he looked at you . . ." She shook her head. "Any rate, the Shore's not a good place, 'specially at night, though I know you kids think it's some sort of amusement park. All the things your dad and me warned you about, they go double, up there. And Hallowe'en's the worst time to go, bar none."

"Because of fairies?"

"Because I say so, miss. Now promise: you go out in *that*—" She nodded at my princess dress, my tinsel crowd, the little mask of tissue-paper veiling I was pinning to it. "—you stay away from there, far as you can get. Or you don't go at all."

"I promise," I said.

"I wish I believed you."

"I *promise,* Grandma."

"Well, it's on you, now. I've said what I could."

And she shrugged, turning back to the stove, where she had biscuits baking. But I could see her eyes were wet.

Why wouldn't you want them to know it was you, though? The fairies? That was what I should have asked—so she could tell me about changelings, or girls caught in rings, boys caught under hills. How time bends in the tunnels, so you might come in one end a child and leave the other an old, old man. How no matter what they serve you, you shouldn't eat, because then it gives them power over you . . . and besides, it's all nothing but dead leaves, really: leaves, and mulch, and bones. Nothing but glamour.

God knows I *would* have asked, had I only known to; just like I wouldn't have done what I did the next night, I'd only known it was a bad idea. But I guess you can say the same about a lot of things.

Heather was a princess for Hallowe'en too, it turned out—a space princess, like from *Star Wars*. Grace was a kitty-cat. And Milton was doubling his fun by wearing a werewolf mask on top of his hockey sweater, so he wouldn't have to choose between the two things he liked best, monsters and sports. "I can play goalie for Frankenstein against Dracula, now," he told us, muffled. "Beat *that*, Barbies!"

He danced with all of us in turn, though, once the music started—and later we all danced with each other, bopping around in tandem to Men With Hats while the big kids passed tissue paper in front of the disco lights to make them strobe. Then grabbed a few Cokes and went outside to cool down, chatting our way past the smokers, the neckers and the scrappers, right to the forest's edge. Which is where Leaf met us.

Not much of a costume, per se—just her usual clothes, threadbare and dusty, so out of fashion they almost looked cool. But she was wearing the best mask I've ever seen bar none, before or since: close-fitted enough you couldn't see any seams, moving with her breath. It had lumpy skin, pale like a potato, a pig's nose and dim little red eyes, and the mouth stretched so far in either direction that if the corners hadn't hit its ears—those lobeless curlicue holes, with their flared and pointed upper ridges of cartilage—it almost looked like they might have just kept on going 'til they met, and the whole top of her head popped off.

"Nuala," she greeted me, her voice hardly even muffled. "And these your friends, of course: Heather . . . Grace. Milton."

Milton didn't quite recoil. "Uh . . . yeah, hi. Nuala, who's this?"

"Leaf," I said. "*You* remember. She's taking us to a party, at her place."

"Leaf who, though?"

I shook my head, only then realizing I'd never actually asked. But: "Redcappie," Leaf replied, without hesitation. "Leaf Redcappie, they call me."

Grace made a little noise. "I have to go home," she said. "Heather—you should come too."

Heather snorted. "What for?"

"*Redcappie*," Grace hissed back, and Heather swallowed, starting as though she'd suddenly remembered something, while Milton and I just watched, confounded.

"Oh yeah," Heather said, at last. "Yeah, we—have fun, you guys."

"Heather?"

She and Grace had already grabbed hands, however, eyes darting, poised to turn. "Have fun," Grace threw back, over her shoulder. "And, um, nice to meet you, Leaf. Tell your folks . . . uh, anyhow."

"*Grace*, what the *spit*, man!"

But they were out of range now, almost out of sight. They didn't look back. Milton and I swapped glances, then looked to Leaf, who didn't seem surprised.

"Wish them good even," she said, "and you two as well, if you'd rather not come with, also. For 'twas good enough to see you the once this night, Nuala, in your guise."

I looked back at Milton, who shrugged. "Let 'em go," he said. "I'm always up for a party, 'specially someplace new. This one's been pretty lame, so far."

Then he smiled at me, so I smiled too—and from the very corner of my eye, I almost thought I saw Leaf smile, even through the skin of her amazing mask. She reached out one hand, and I took it.

Into the woods we went, all three—but when November finally dawned, on the cold hill's side, only one of us came back.

I remember waking up, on my back, covered with dew. I was cold, and my eyes hurt. I think I'd been crying.

I remember stumbling home, through the woods. Crawling back through the hedge, so clumsy I tore myself on its twigs.

I remember what Dad's face looked like, when he opened the door and found me wavering there. My grandmother sitting at the kitchen table, face in her hands, her shoulders shaking.

Heather and Grace came to visit me in the hospital, two days later, and stood looking at me for a long minute, still hand in hand, like they'd never broken apart in the last seventy-two hours.

"We thought you'd be okay, is all," Heather said, finally. "You guys. Because you knew her."

"Uh huh," I replied, voice slow and grating, through my swollen throat. "I . . . *thought* I did, yeah."

"So what happened?" Grace asked. "To Milton?"

" . . . Don't know."

And after we'd all taken a few minutes to digest that: "Well," she couldn't quite stop herself from saying. "You know that's your *fault,* right?"

(Right.)

Once I was well enough to travel, my dad finally left Overdeere again, taking me with him. We moved first to God's Lips, then Barrie (ironically enough), then Mississauga, then Toronto proper. I graduated high school there, made Ontario Scholar, got into U of T. My grandmother was dead by that time, of course; she left everything to Dad, who left it in turn to me, as I only discovered after he had a fatal heart attack earlier this year.

I majored in History, with a minor in Library Sciences that I parlayed into my own personal line of research. Eventually, I stumbled upon the Connaught Trust, where the records that had eluded me thus far are kept. Which is how, years on, I learned the truth behind the Dourvale Shore's legendary reputation—about those three bloodlines of Overdeere which supposedly trace themselves back to Scotland, to the fairies, each family's lineage weaving back and forth and in and out of the others' like worms through a dead dog's heart: the Druirs of Stane Hill, lofty and secret, plus their descendants the Sidderstanes, who lend their name to the Cannery, and own most of Overdeere proper. Not to mention the poorest of all their many poor relations, the Redcappies.

Though few of this latter clan have ever been seen in town, they did once own a set of houses in Dourvale in 1935, before the development collapsed, leaving the village untenanted and derelict. And this also happens to be when the youngest Redcappie family member was a nine-year-old girl named Duille, which—in Scots Gaelic—means "Leaf."

Old, old, her voice sighs through my head sometimes, at night, when I'm alone. *Old, I am, and so strange. Like beer brewed in an eggshell.*

But that's not the whole of it, not yet.

Roughly a year after that Hallowe'en, two hunters tracking a downed duck found the hairy tip of a werewolf mask's ear poking up out of the sod on Stane Hill. Their dog began to whine and dig at it, and as they struggled to pull him away, one hunter felt rather than heard a faint, erratic knocking from beneath their feet. Ten minutes of frenzied excavation later, they broke through a blister in the earth and uncovered a thin, dirty boy in a hockey sweater, his mask's orifices clogged with dirt. When he finally stopped crying and screaming, he told them his name was Milton Recamier, and that he thought he'd been trapped down there for a few days. Maybe a week.

The authorities said he must have fallen into a Hell Hole and been trapped underground, but Milton claimed he'd been stuck inside the Hill itself, breathing its rock like air. Unsurprisingly, he quickly ended up in a mental institution, where he stayed until he changed his tune.

When we were both sixteen, I was visiting friends in God's Lips when he suddenly walked up to me on the street. He looked ragged, literally and figuratively, with a weird sort of eczema at his temples that I later realized might have been the result of electroshock therapy.

"She told me to give this to you, if I saw you again," he said, handing me a package.

"Who?"

"Leaf."

It was an old paper bag, opening folded and scotch-taped to create a seal, and by the time I'd unwrapped it, he was already too far away to call after him, even if I'd been capable. Instead, I just looked down, frozen, my chest hot and hollow. Because what it held was—a knot of ribbon.

Green.

Trimmed in silver foil.

The kind my mother was wearing, the day she left.

—⌘—

I'd help you if I could, Nuala. For that you're my friend. My one. My only.

—⌘—

So little of that night I recall, still, at all. Shreds and patches.

Inside Leaf's relatives' house—the Hill?—it was bright (dark), and hot (cold), full of figures (yes) in costume (no), adults and children (maybe), men and women (likewise); I remember shouldering my way through a crowd of whirling, laughing, dancing creatures, humming along and toe-tapping to music I thought I recognized somehow, even though I was equally sure I'd never heard it before. Milton was spun off, whirling away through the darkness, borne on the riotous tide; Leaf clutched me close and let him go, pulling me past reams of food spread out on tables, glistening and delicious-smelling, a feast for the ages. (But: *Don't eat any, Nuala, not one bite,* I felt her say, right into my ear's hiddenmost whorls, so they vibrated secretly. *It will do you no good, if you ever wish to leave here.*)

Milton, in the distance, was cramming his face, with both hands. He looked like he enjoyed it, at the time, and whenever I think about it now, I really hope he did.

"Have to sit down," I told her, indistinctly, to which she shook her head: "Nay, but keep on, I pray—slack not, 'tis only a little way farther. We're almost through."

Pulling me on, on, ever on, past men with horns and girls with tails, faces with two mouths, faces with none. Eyes and teeth and glittering scales, leaves and vines and fruit blooming straight from skin, crowns of candles lit like marsh-flame, guttering in the darkness. Past the flap of wings and the brachiating leap of things high above, hurling themselves back and forth as though from branch to branch in some massive, invisible copse of trees.

And then, suddenly, in the very midst of it all—a dark young man, blue-eyed and handsome, emerged full-blown, coming toward us through the crowd. Leaf tried her best to avoid him, but he eddied forward, blooming up between us with his arms crossed, frowning down. And I saw (*thought* I saw) that when he blinked, his lids—long-lashed, luxuriant, shadow-touched at their rims, as though lined with kohl—shut the wrong way 'round entirely: not from the top, down, but from the bottom, up.

"Cousin Saracen," Leaf murmured, masked head suddenly hunched, as if she feared to be hit. And: "Leaf," he said, his voice strongly Scots-burred, original template to her merest imitation, "what is't ye've done, my poor, small fool? Tae bring *this* one here, tonight . . ."

"I thought to show her, only. Only that."

"Ye should not have, as well ye know."

"Yet she's blood, kin—Jess Nuttall's girl's boy. You remember, aye? And . . . my friend, also."

"That's no account of mine, girl. Ye know my mother's views."

"But—"

He waved her protest away. "Show her the whole truth, Leaf, then loose her tae go, while she still can. Bid her see straight what she half-glimpses already, and let that be an end on't."

"And what of her company?"

"Him? Oh, he's e'en now caught, mazed fast; our families must have their will of him, to work away his debt. No concern of either of ours, therefore—not like her."

Leaf sighed. "I know it," she said, softer still, almost into her neck.

And . . . first we were standing there, then we weren't, swerved sidelong into some smaller chamber all filled with moss and apples, sticky-sweet and vaguely rot-stinking. By my foot, the pale flower of some woman's hand reached up from farther down, submerged below the wrist in the rocky floor, splayed fingers discolored by decay.

"Don't look there," Leaf told me, raising my head by the chin, as my vision swam. "Here, Nuala, best of all friends. Look to me, only. Look to me."

And her mouth opened, the mask's mouth, wide and wider, wider still. 'Til it seemed the entire top of her potato-pale skull might tip back, drop free and roll away, leaving her nothing but teeth and tongue, gaped open wetly to the world. Except . . .

. . . it wasn't a mask, of course. At all. Just her, the real her, finally visible, without the lies. Without—

—"The glamour."

I don't know what I said. What noises I might have been making. Which is odd, because I know for sure that I could hear *her*—Leaf, bending in above me herself as her cousin watched, lowering herself so we were eye to eye once more, where I crouched gibbering on that half-rotten, hand-flowered floor. Saying, sadly, as she did:

"Tonight we guise no more, for 'tis the time of it—this one night of all the year, when we may walk abroad unremarked-on, wearing our own faces in jest as we cannot, any other time, or risk a broken covenant. And I did so want you to see me true, if only for the once."

I gaped, and she sighed, and her cousin reached out a six-fingered hand to my shoulder, pushing me out through the Hill's wall. I saw the roots and stones rush by me, *through* me, sifting my very atoms, resistlessly as rain. And then it was dawn, the cold light of day, and I was lying staring up into the sky, my spine hurting, every bone in my body lit up with what seemed like one single, awful ache.

They still ache like that, sometimes, even now. That's when I know I'm seeing something I should probably pay attention to.

Here are some things I believe, now, though I have little or no proof for them:

My mother is probably the tree they found her purse in, hands upflung into pleading branches like Daphne, with bark growing over every part of her. Or maybe she's a stone instead, standing frozen somewhere on Dourvale's streets, with only the sun crawling across her skin to tell her time is passing. Maybe she's buried in Stane Hill, same as Milton once was, except farther down. One way or the other, I don't expect to find her alive. I don't expect to *find* her, not even if I was to finally start looking.

At Stane Hill, the Druirs' seat, Leaf touched me to get me in, not that she probably needed to, and I touched Milton to get him in, not knowing he wouldn't be able to leave without me 'til he'd worked off the food he took. Blood opens the door, you see—both ways, probably.

The older I get, the more I watch Leaf's cousin surface in me—handsome Saracen with his poison-blue eyes, eternally young and unspeakably old, who once carved his name on a table to impress my grandmother, back when she was still sweet young Jess Nuttall. I sit in my apartment with my part-fairy bones aching, off and on, longing for my great-grandfather's hedgerow, the hole beneath and the woods beyond. It's my inheritance, after all.

We have the stink of humanity on us, we quarterlings, too much so for the eldest of our blood to ever find us sweet, Leaf's voice whispers to me sometimes, late at night, whether I'm dreaming or awake. *The hills will not open for us; the rings are closed forever. Who can we turn to, therefore, except each other? Which is why no one will ever be coming for you but me, Nuala, just as no one will ever be coming for me, in the end, but . . . probably, possibly, if I only wait long enough . . .*

(Oh, how I hope, my dearest, my only friend. Oh, how I pray.)

. . . you.

I *know* myself now, you see, at last. I'm no monster; not that Leaf was one either, not entirely. But in one particular, I agree with her, completely: This Iron World hurts me, and I'm tired of guising. I want to take off my false face and see the one beneath, maybe the same one I used to draw, over and over: wrinkled like a nut, peeled like birch. And one day soon . . .

. . . *very* soon, most likely, given it's October again, and Hallowe'en draws near . . .

. . . I will.

GUISING: A COMMENTARY

THIS DELIGHTFULLY DEVIOUS WORK OF DARK fantasy indulges what the title promises: it's all about dis*guise*. Or rather, "guising"—a Briticism for ritual masking—here practiced in the realm of fae, and here set in North Ontario. The story has a strong sense of place, despite being so make-believe, perhaps reflecting in some ways Files's own upbringing and experiences and dreams. Dark as her fiction tends to be, here we have fun and funny fairies—*from Hell*—operating in their own shadow realm (underfoot—accessed from the "Hell Holes" that Grandmother warns our protagonist about). The world of fae in Files's hands is not some simple alternative reality; it is far too much for the "normal" world to comprehend without mental breakdown, save for the narrator, who is revealed to be a quarterling, a being partly made of fairy blood, after all. Thus, like some of the other stories in this collection, the fae world is a frightening place—yet one where the narrator discovers her destiny.

"Guising" is a complex contribution to the "Halloween horror" subgenre, but it is much more than just a tale of masquerade or trick-or-treat. Like many of Files's stories, this tale is rife with folkloric sources that few writers can delve into so deeply, and her playful reference to archetypes, legends, and mythlore dominates the reader's experience in a singular and unforgettable manner. Her talent for realizing both historically distant times and psychologically rich (and nightmarish) imaginary realms is fully on display as the narrator explores the forest and bonds with her newfound friend, "guised" to pass as best as a fairy can as ordinary in the ordinary world.

It is a tale, moreover, of a kind of sisterhood, and a kind of coming-of-age that feels distinctively feminine, as the males of the story recede or are weakened by their exposure to the fae world, even as the main fairy and "human" protagonist bond and learn the "truth" of their common history. Thus, to a degree, the patriarchal world is unmasked and civilization mocked in this piece, rendered as broken as Milton becomes when things go topsy-turvy. While it is a little reductive to suggest that this is simply a feminist revision of folklore, Files does such things often, and here she plays artfully with language and storytelling in a meta-fictional way, calling attention to the limitations of language and the "official" ways in which stories are told. Language hides and reveals. And the truth cannot be found in the law and order of the "civilized" world. Here all truth is unmasked in the glamour.

—Michael Arnzen, PhD

YOL

YOU'VE ASKED ME HOW IT CAME ABOUT THAT our family were eventually converted to the new faith of Christianity, having hitherto been proud farmers who went viking at their jarl's command and only worshipped the Norse gods, Odin, Thor, Freyr, and Freya in particular. This is that story.

At that time, we lived on a farm near Kjartanholt, on the peninsula of Snaefellsnes, where many ghostly doings have been recorded in various sagas. Similar things had of course happened near us as well, tales my father and uncles often took great glee in the telling: of how a whale beached itself once on the sands near where my mother and I gathered gulls' eggs, for example, after which a fight broke out between two groups of men who assembled to flense the whale, and several men were killed. One lived long enough after his leg was cut off to curse the man who dealt him that blow, who happened to be my youngest uncle, Thorolf Red-Hair.

That night, after a great dealt of drinking and celebration, Thorolf wandered away, and a week later he was found on the same sands where the man who cursed him's blood had fallen, black from head to toe and with all his bones broken. Nor did the curse end there, for from that day forth my uncle Thorolf haunted our homestead, wandering over the hills and causing mischief, as if he and we had never been related by blood. Eventually, my father was forced to dig Thorolf up and bury him again under a cairn of rune stones, which at least kept him from walking, though the land around his cairn became useless as pasture, since any sheep who slept over his grave would inevitably be found dead in the morning.

Now one year, as the festival of Yol approached, we heard much talk about how Snorri the Priest had apparently become Christian, and was proclaiming that all of Snaelfellsnes should become Christian likewise. At one time Snorri and Arnkel of Holyfell had striven together, sharing the title of jarl, but Snorri had since killed Arnkel and become sole possessor of the jarlhold, to which my family was sworn. So on the night before the festival itself, my father and his brothers met to discuss whether or not they too should become Christians, if Snorri required it of them. This was an idea to which my eldest uncle, Geirrod, objected strenuously.

"I do not wish to insult our gods," he said, "who are both powerful and alive, on behalf of a god who is surely some sort of *draug*, given that he is said to be a dead man slain like a thief who somehow came back to life yet remains nailed to a cross made from wood. Not to mention how he has since caused the death of many, not through his own strength—like Thor or Odin—but by slyly whispering in the ears of Frankian or English monks, who then tell their kings who he wants them to kill in his name."

"Our priests also give advice, when asked," my father said, "as do our seers." To which my uncle answered: "Yes, but because they well know the thread of our fate is already spun, they do not expect us to do anything except by our own decision. Whatever we choose, we will arrive at the same end soon enough."

"I have heard that this Christ is the son of a greater god still," my mother put in, "which is likely enough—indeed, at this time of year, he is worshipped mainly as the baby he once was, born on Yol-tide. Christ's Mass, they call it. Yet I have also heard he is not only that god's son but the god himself, somehow, and that his mother was a virgin both when she conceived him and after his birth, which is an obviously ridiculous idea."

There was more talk after this, but I was a child, and had already drunk much mead. So I do not recall exactly when it was that I fell asleep, only that I woke later on, in the very dead of night. All about me, my elders were likewise deeply aslumber, some of them naked and rolled in furs, having given themselves over to revelry; my little brothers and elder sister were curled around me in a pile, snoring. It was cold outside, the snow having begun to fall when our meal first commenced, but inside it was warm and stinking. It was familiar. It was home.

Slowly, however, I saw something take shape outside, a blue-white half-moon of light that wavered in the air and turned the falling snow to sparks around it—bright sparks to each side and gray sparks behind, almost black, as if it were not snow that fell, but ash.

At first I thought it was a corpse-candle of the sort that sometimes form near the summer solstice, and can be followed by those brave enough, leading them to buried treasure. Then I thought perhaps it might be a weird-moon instead, a sign of deaths to follow, for my uncle Geirrod had told me once how he saw one enter into the great fire-hall at Frodis-water, circling backward and widdershins around the tables before going back out again, only to return every night thereafter until all the village's men went out to fish and never returned, except as dripping ghosts. And eventually, the matter was only settled once the dead men were given a door-doom that barred them from ever returning.

But this was not either of those things, as it happens. This was like nothing I had ever seen, before or since.

Bright and black and cold, the light outside came closer still, eddying through the door. It cast itself upon the earthen floor, the tables and furs, the faces of my kin. I saw them frown and grimace under its touch; here and there I watched eyes open and narrow, seeking for the source. And then the light which had been like a half-moon blinked likewise, opening itself further, the way a lid does, to disclose something entirely else that had all the time lain behind it.

Of *draugr*, we say they are blue-skinned, dark, and awful. This child—this *baby*—was much the same, though also red in places; red-dripping from the cord looped around its waist to dangle slack between its equal-slack legs, floating above where the fire-coals smoldered; red-pink and crusted white across its face, bearing a caul such as our seers and those gods-chosen are often born with.

Its pudgy hands crossed at its breastbone, tiny fingers curled. Its eyes shut, yet glowing. The whole of it glowing brighter and brighter. Shedding molten gold like heavy rain.

My father jumped up, grabbing for his sword; my uncle Geirrod drew his hand-axe and struck hard at this dreadful thing, cleaving it straight through the skull. For a moment the split face opened its eyes, looking straight at me, or seeming to; I saw those lids lift beneath the caul, the eyes themselves gold as well, while the half-brain thus exposed flared like the sun just risen does as it breaks horizon. I heard my uncle Geirrod scream, dropping the axe, which smoked as though pulled forth from a forge. I saw his strong hand curl and melt together, instantly crippled, scar forming to scar.

And when my father struck to avenge him, sword spearing in through that blazing creature's soft stomach, he roared and let it go as soon as the heat touched him, for which he took almost no harm beyond a blister. Then we watched his sword melt from whatever ran through the thing's guts like blood—that fire, that *power*. Right in front of us, hot enough to brand, and make, and kill: There, *real*. Undeniable, in a way no thunder of Thor's distant hammer could ever be.

I heard a voice in my head then, gold as well, and clarion, a blown battle horn. Behind the floating child I saw wings, beating. The shadow of a cross suggesting the child grown to full strength, arms spread to accept iron nails, a crown of bloody thorns settling onto its brow. The cross planted deep in a mountain of skulls, and its shadow spilling out over the whole world.

See, now: By the strength of my Father and in His secret, unspeakable Name, I am born from death, again and again, this voice seemed to tell me—to tell us all. *A plant born from no seed; a seed needing no soil, no sun, no tending. Thus you cannot defeat me, for nothing that now lives can destroy what I am.*

Your gods must die, as all do. But I do not.

I cannot.

I am a marvel, a fearful thing. Worship me. Fear me.

Gloria in excelsis deo . . . meo.

Gloria.

I heard my mother weeping, then, my sister and brothers too. In understanding. In shame, and joy, and fear.

And when Yol broke the morning after, we lit our fires as always, gathered boughs of pine and plaited them in wreaths, painted our faces with blood and crushed berries. And when we had drunk enough to risk it, to dare to, we threw the images of our gods upon the pyre and let them burn to ash. And the next week we went up to Holyfell and pledged ourselves to Snorri the Priest once more, this time as Christians.

And nothing happened.

We still went viking, we still killed, still drank, still took thralls, still sold them as slaves and sired children on them; we still shed blood, though this time in Jesus the Christ's name. Sometimes we slew each other, and paid blood-gelt for it. Sometimes we knelt and prayed, did penance, were forgiven. Once we'd yearned for Valhalla, and some did yet (I have no doubt), though out loud they called it Heaven.

But we never saw that child again, at least.

And for that, I am thankful.

YOL:
A COMMENTARY

FILES GIVES US A DISTINCTIVE HOLIDAY STORY, inviting the reader to consider the early days of "Yule" through the eyes of an early day Viking tribe. The story overtly flips Christmas lore on its head, using horror imagery to directly subvert any modern-day preconceptions of the Christ child one might harbor. The child of God here is omnipotent and for Files that means it is also truly frightening. The result is a story that reminds us—entirely as much as the primitives whose viewpoint control the tale—that a religious experience must by definition break our brain's hold on not just "reality" but also all the cultural assumptions that are barnacled onto that concept of reality.

This is also a great example of Files's ability to take any common genre theme and spin it her own way, often with a dark wink or impish chuckle. "Yol" is a brilliant contribution to the subgenre known as Christmas horror (one made popular by

Charles Dickens, and which remains such with recent published anthologies and films like *Black Christmas*). "Yol" is also a very dark joke mocking the whole holiday itself, and I suspect readers—whether they find its transgressive humor hilarious or not—will never forget it come December. This story is a gift.

—Michael Arnzen, PhD

Why Gemma Files Matters

by Michael Arnzen, PhD

GEMMA FILES IS A HORROR AUTHOR CELEBRATED for any number of reasons—from her breakthrough novels that bend gender and genre alike (her Hexslinger horror western fantasies take a hemispherical approach to the idea of "Western" and feature gay characters without lowering them to mere tokens); to her penchant for cinema and its history (as in her lauded book, *Experimental Film*, or her chilling erotic horror stories in *The Hunger* TV series). Her skills as a folklorist are self-evident in her approach to fabulist writing, bringing to life history and myth and cultures beyond our knowledge . . . no matter how imaginary, her voice and her prose make her worlds feel so real; the diversity of subjects she has taken on across her oeuvre are nothing short of astounding. She can do so much, so well, because she is hyperaware of her own interstitiality, and is especially intimate with her dark side. Files has an uncanny knack for adopting the viewpoints of the historically distant, the profoundly unimaginable, or the unfairly marginalized, and framing them with themes of existential dread and moral revenge. And yet at her foundation she is a historicist who knows her research on top of simply being a fantastic storyteller who respects and empowers the voices of cultural others across the board.

In a word, Gemma *represents*.

Gemma Files is also a *challenging* writer, on multiple levels, and her refusal to accept simplicity, boundary lines, and the definition of reality by social forces, is precisely what makes her so damned intriguing. She's intelligent, well-read, deviously witty, and incredibly savvy about folklore and archetype that she wields these impulses and braids them together effortlessly in her fiction. Her "trick"—if such a word applies—is being able to occupy the unfamiliar viewpoint in any situation, often of the outsider looking in, which in turn chimes with the *stranger inside ourselves*. Like a true fantasist, she remains unsettled with givens, especially those that might "define" reality. But Gemma is darker than Gene Wolfe, more cynical than Neil Gaiman. She's like a vampire Franz Kafka in drag, giving other dark auteurs who love to tap into folklore and myth (like, say, Tim Powers, who excels at this kind of thing) a run for their money. Files matters because she always comes at time-tested tropes from a unique (often marginalized) angle that interrogates those very same tropes, or otherwise exploits them in a vivid way that generates a sense of awe, or sublime wonder or dark dread. In the process she problematizes our assumptions, using the shock and gore of horror to probe them so effectively that readers rethink them in a transformative way.

Gemma Files deserves the attention she's been getting

lately, in literary awards and through the praise of her peers and readers alike, because she was far ahead of her time, even when she was first getting started. She's been challenging patriarchal complacency roughly since her story "Skeleton Bitch" appeared in the hard-to-find but essential literary horror magazine of the mid-'90s, *Palace Corbie*. That tale was perhaps the first I'd ever read that dared to put the word "bitch" right in the title (and years before Meredith Brooks's infamous song), and it *got me* with its genuine dread and terror, framed in a way that made me sit up and take notice. I instantly knew a fearless feminist was at work in the field, one as provocative as Billy Martin (Poppy Z. Brite, at the time) and that she had as much to say about culture-at-large as she did about the human body and desire. As she delved into novels and longer stories in the decades that followed, she became one of the first and best to bring mythology and the wild west into concert with horror fiction, with an openly gay cast of characters, no less, in her *Hexslinger* series. Creatively restless, she's become a pioneer of hybrid fantasy fiction, queer writing, cosmic horror, and Canadian folk horror. Gemma Files means serious business and loves to feature protagonists who fuck with the worlds they inhabit, often in a witty, defiant way, and in my view that's an extension of what she herself is trying to do with her writing. And she does it so well.

The stories selected for this collection reveal the diversity of Files's fiction quite well, but in my view nothing is more revelatory of her talent than the Robert Chambers-inspired tale, "Slick Black Bones and Soft Black Stars," an homage which fits firmly into the mythos of *The King in Yellow*, while extending its terrifying implications. Here, Files really gets at the alterity of Carcosa—the pure and frightening otherness of this unimaginable place—and is a good test case for looking at how Gaytari Spivak's theory of "the subaltern" plays out in her hands.

Spivak essentially explored the way that those who do not qualify for citizenship in a society are culturally oppressed as being simultaneously (sub-) *beneath* and (-altern) *different* than the dominant, mainstream social classes, and how this segment of society are not only both literally and figuratively "down and out" but also kept in that position, subjugated and treated as non-human for the "crime" of simply not fitting in. In fact, keeping these people oppressed and "in their place" functions to empower their oppressors, who construct a system of oppression to maintain *their* place in relationship to them. Often these are the people who are colonized by some superpower, and one need only think about how Native Americans and indigenous tribes across the Western Hemisphere were treated by settlers from Europe to understand this concept. Spivak's theory extends that historical treatment into the politics of everyday life today, in which power continues to repeat the logic of the colonizer in post-modern life, often unthinkingly. Indeed, the repressed and neglected guilt of the oppressive colonizer only comes back to haunt them, bafflingly, often in ways they can't comprehend or understand. Files's fiction seems hyperaware of the post-colonial identity politics that play out in the world today, and in the days of yore.

We see find this concept lurking right under the graveyard sand in "Slick Black Bones and Soft Black Stars," which adopts a folk horror narrative to adapt Chambers's concepts and update them in a contemporary manner. Many works of the "folk horror" subgenre seem to reflect post-colonial guilt, where visitors from a modern culture (sometimes on research expeditions, sometimes on tourist jaunts) are interlopers on foreign soil. Sometimes, like the proverbial "ugly Amercian," these outlanders are brash in trampling upon that soil, patting locals on the head or treating them like servants to their whims, and we root for the local "primitives" to get their revenge on them for their egotism and arrogance. In "Slick Black Bones," the stakes are higher. In this story, mankind itself is served a cold dish of revenge, and beneath all the tropes of horror, what amounts to a cultural uprising is staged.

Yes, at its core, "Slick Black Bones" is a story about a resurrecting god—the King in Yellow, pieced together one-by-one by the bones that the tribal residents of the isle of Carcosa are replicating inside of them. Files's ingenious plot conceit is remarkable in and of itself, and produces that frisson of terror that readers are expecting from a story like this, when the narrator falls into the grave in which the skeleton of the god is rebuilding itself of mold-like flesh, bullet-ridden and bleeding. Her blood feeds the god, helping it complete its final moment of resurrection (and therefore leading to the narrator's salvation when the King promises, "almost affectionately ... to take [her] home." But what's important to underscore here is the clever way in which the King is not a single individual monarch, but essentially a *mosaic of its people*, literally a collective body, patchworked together over time by their blood and bones.

Files cleverly does not merely assert the power of the subaltern people of Carcosa. She also converts the narrator, who transitions into alien in the end. Earlier in the story, the translator Ringo asks the invasive archaeology group to "take me with you" as a favor if they can escape the island, and in a brilliant turn of events, no one escapes at all and the people take the narrator with them, literally embodied by the King, instead. In death, but further, in the surrender of her identity as an individual, she metaphorically has joined their collective and has become subaltern alongside them.

In her work on the "subaltern," Spivak suggests an existential divide does indeed exist between the colonialist and the colonized, and warns Western thinkers from purporting to truly understand the experience of the Other, since we are so immersed in our own hierarchies and customs that we may not be able to really listen or comprehend, and may remake them as our own in the process. There's a degree to which Files's ending—as dark as it is (and it can't get much darker, dying paralyzed by gory gunfire and literally facing a re-animating corpse) is ironically *optimistic*, therefore, not merely because the narrator survives, but because she overcomes that existential divide and loses her Western sense of self and superiority completely, joining the culture spiritually in the story's conclusion. It is, perhaps, the ideal ending too, for a student of the grave to truly become one with the skeletal remains she has studied all her life. Thus, as much as the story describes a loss of identity and a loss of life, there is at the same time a kind of self-actualization happening here: perhaps she has identified with the subaltern on some level, all along. Letting go of her Western ways allows her to fully realize who she is and—as the King's words suggest—allows this nomad researcher to return "home."

And perhaps so it is with the reader, too, who through character identification is brought face-to-face with an extreme otherness that lurks inside of us. Gemma Files matters because she brings the subaltern to life, giving them a voice which—while alien, distant, or inaccessibly Other—we somehow have access to through the vehicle of the fantastic.

Gemma Files *represents*, even when what she's presenting us is unrepresentable.

BELOVED
HUSBAND

In Conversation with Gemma Files

ERIC J. GUIGNARD: Hi Gemma, and great to chat with you here. I've been a fan of your short fiction ever since I read "The Emperor's Old Bones" in Ellen Datlow and Terri Windling's *The Year's Best Fantasy & Horror: Thirteenth Annual Collection* (the 626-page hardback version—it weighs over three pounds!). That was followed soon after by "Kissing Carrion" in Stephen Jones's *The Mammoth Book of Best New Horror 15*, and then years later and most definitely with "Nanny Grey" (still an absolute favorite) and "Satan's Jewel Crown" and "Slick Black Bones and Soft Black Stars" (included in this primer). I can say that I've been reading your work for over two decades, and I still get very excited when I come across a new piece of your writing touted in an upcoming anthology or magazine issue.

And you've been writing for publication even before that; "Fly-by-Night" was your first fiction publication credit, a vampire tale in 1993, so you've over thirty years of involvement in this genre. How has your growth as a writer changed during that time? Do you feel that you've evolved with the Horror-Dark Fantasy market or do you write what you wish, and let it land wherever it will? Tell us a little about the themes and topics you put forth when you first started out, as compared to what you write now.

Gemma Files: Hm. Well, when I first started writing I was still pretty firmly involved in what a *Locus* magazine interviewer called "The Sex and Death Show" . . . my stuff was definitely hornier and far more explicitly angry, though not exactly angri*er*, per se. More explicit in every way, I think. Laird Barron called me a punk when he read my first two collections, and sometimes I'm not so sure I'm exactly that anymore. But then again, what else would I be? I'm Gen X, born in 1968, literally on the day Martin Luther King, Jr. was assassinated. I grew up under the impending impression that these were End Times, only to later realize that all times are occupied by both endings and beginnings. Or maybe nothing really ever ends, and all those "sad but necessary" decisions we make thinking that only Last Things matter are equally likely to be stuff we were always looking for an excuse to do anyhow.

One way or the other, it's taken me a very long time to reconcile with the fact that I really do have a right to feel traumatized, just like everyone else. When I was younger, I thought Rage Against (Whatever) was an energy, and it is, but it's also a drug, a form of self-medication; it'll wear you right out, grind you down so fine that everything hurts, that pain and pleasure become indistinguishable. I have to pace myself now, because I have people who depend on me, so I can't run myself ragged anymore. And this knowledge has perhaps since made it into my fiction as a certain understanding that staying alive might sometimes be harder than dying, especially if you're doing it for others; that going against your own instincts might be more admirable than totally indulging your own selfish desires, your perverse flailing after a way to explode and take the universe with you, your monster pride epiphany . . . in long-form narratives, at least. Because one of the true joys of short fiction is that you can kill everybody and then kill yourself, laughing hysterically, and make it look like victory.

I've never had much success chasing the market, even on those few occasions when I've tried, so yeah, I do pretty much write what I want and let other people tell me if it's their jam or not. In a lot of ways, I think that finding what you're best at and doing it 'til the wheels come off is all that any creative artist can offer—we're taught to think it's self-indulgent to go where our tastes take us, but I continue to believe that indulging yourself isn't so bad, as long as you set standards and go about meeting them professionally. One thing I'm happy to have discovered over these last thirty years is that I *do* have fans, I do have an audience—at least one young writer told me that an early story of mine told her she really could do exactly what she wanted to without it blowing up in her face, so thanks for that. "Oh, I'm so glad!" I replied. "Which story was that?" "'Kissing Carrion,'" she told me, proudly, so . . . yeah, that makes me happy in a very weird way, given what said story is about. If you know, you know.

EJG: Your story "Sown from Salt" is a great dive into the Weird Western genre with biblical reflections, haunted spirits, and gunslingin' revenge. It's a popular set-up you've used, essentially "a stranger walks into town," but ratcheted up to turn this Clint Eastwood-like character into the Angel of Death.

"Sown from Salt" and its sequel "A Feast for Dust" have intricate worldbuilding and mythology woven throughout, and it plays well on so many levels. You've also published the *Hexslinger* trilogy of novels (plus some other connected *Hexslinger* work) that are Weird Westerns with similar themes of tragic love and retribution, instilling dark magic into frontier towns. What attracts you to this genre, which is so unlike much of your other work (nautical mythology, haunted films, sinister Cthulhu-esque fantasy, etc.)? Will gunman Reese ever cross paths against Ed Morrow or Asher Rook or the other *Hexslinger* brigands/Pinkerton detectives?

GF: In retrospect, I guess that Sartain Stannard Reese might have been a bit of a rehearsal for Chess Pargeter, though I do think "Sown From Salt" and "A Feast For Dust" don't entirely inhabit the Hexslinger 'verse, even if the apparently-unrelated story "Satan's Jewel Crown" (reprinted in *Drawn Up From Deep Places*) definitely does. Anyhow, yeah—what *do* I love most about the Western? Probably that it reminds me a lot of the roaming outlaw narratives of the Fantasy/Sword & Sorcery weird stories I grew up reading, from Tanith Lee and Marion Zimmer Bradley to Michael Moorcock to Robert E. Howard; it's frontier-set, tribal, a great place for characters who don't fit in to ramble and rumble in. Thanks to these similarities, I got to know the *Yojimbo/Red Harvest* template a long time before I encountered either that particular movie or book proper, and the wild, alien, dangerous nature of the Western landscape makes it a wonderful place for various different sorts of faith to merge into outright magic, as we see with tales as apparently disparate as those of Solomon Kane and Silver John. Not to mention that the first poems I loved were all murder ballads, so that helps as well. I can't ever see myself completely letting go of this mythology, or any other type.

EJG: As an instructor through the online writers' community LitReactor, you've spoken before on adding believability to stories by "writing about the weird things that actually occur in one's life." What's the weirdest thing that's occurred to you that has made its way into your writing?

GF: What I'm more in favor of is taking a bit of grit from life and forming a pearl of weird around it—not so much "that was so strange" as "man, what if that had been a *lot* stranger?" I don't feel like my life's been very weird overall, but then again, I'm always being confronted with moments that were normal to me when I was inside them that turn out to strike other people as very *not* normal, comparatively.

For example: One time my mom was at an acting class and the fuses blew at our place. I was stuck on the front hall steps, frozen, unable to get myself to go down to the basement and reset them. I phoned her, panicked, and she said, "Okay, I'm coming home, but my scene partner will probably get there before me—just let him in and he'll work it out." A bit later the doorbell rings. I open the door and find Darryl Revok from *Scanners* (Michael Ironside) standing on the porch. "Hi," he says. "I'm your Mom's friend Mike, I'm here to change the fuses." Which is one reason why old Cronenberg films always remind me of my childhood.

EJG: Besides short fiction, novels, and essays, you also have published poetry for over twenty years. How is it different for you in the mindset of writing poetry rather than other styles of writing (i.e. prose or non-fiction)? Do you draw from the same muse? You also have experience with screenwriting, journalism, critical reviewing, and more. Is there any style of writing you avoid or dislike?

GF: In a lot of ways, I think poetry is the most instinctual way I process things, emotionally. For me, the trio of Canadian poets who primarily taught me how to change an internal monologue or series of observations into a poem are Gwendolyn MacEwen, Susan Musgrave, and Pat Lowther. All of them were/are obsessed with sex, death, mythology, archaeology, language, and history, so I connected with them in that way—they became sort of examples to live up to for me, "saints," as the *Heavenly Creatures* girls might say.

MacEwen drank herself to death, but she also taught herself to read and write in Egyptian hieroglyphics, and once she was a Catholic schoolgirl at the same school my Mom went to; they'd turn their backs on the school and light up, secure in the knowledge that they weren't smoking "within sight" of it. Susan Musgrave married a bank robber/author who broke out of jail and wrote a book about it. Pat Lowther's husband beat her to death with a hammer, probably because he was jealous of her writing skills, and a man my mom dated later adapted a book-length poem one of her students wrote about her murder into a radio show. All of these stories told me that you could take your life and break it down for parts and make something out of it, first as poetry, then as fiction. No wonder I've been so often accused of committing poetic purple prose.

Regarding the second part of your question, I made a decision a while back not to write about stuff I don't enjoy unless someone's paying me for it; does that count? No, for me writing is like breathing—even the boring stuff is necessary, if you want to stay alive. I've got *Harriet the Spy* disease; notes, or it didn't happen.

EJG: How vibrant is Canada's horror community? Who are other Canadian horror writers you might recommend, or who have influenced you; or projects or events you might suggest fans seek?

GF: Short answer, very. Long answer . . .

When I first started writing I felt as if I had to continually kick against the idea that Canada was by definition a substandard copy of something else—Europe when I was younger (mosaic instead of melting pot, the UK as model for English-speaking Canada, France for French-speaking), then increasingly the U.S. ("I kinda thought this movie was pretty good, until I figured out it was *Canadian*," my students would complain, when I was still teaching at film school.) We had "no history," or so we told ourselves, but that was never actually true—we just didn't tell each other about it or tried to forget it. It was my very Australian dad, for example, who first told me that the Upper and Lower Canada Rebellions of 1837/38 against the British Empire sent completely French-speaking Quebecois people into the Tasmanian penal system. Later, when I looked for one textbook to teach Canadian film history from, I had to Frankenstein a bunch of them together myself—our sense of ourselves has always been self-deprecating and anecdata-driven, even when we're talking about nightmares and dreamscapes. Magic realism? Sure—you can win prizes with *that*. Horror? Move down south and get your Green Card if that's the sort of populist crap you want to make money off of, you fake-ass hoser!

Thankfully, things have definitely changed since I once thought I was being *super* daring to actually set stuff in the city I lived in (Toronto), as opposed to doing the runaway production vs. prose version of hanging Mardi Gras beads all over Market Street and pretending it was New Orleans … and you know what? I kind of think that writing horror has a lot to do with being willing to name and shame yourself, in that particular way. You're a weirdo no matter what when you write horror, so why not also be loud and proud about being queer, or Indigenous, or hyphenated in any other sort of way (from *this* province, from *this* culture, from *this* background, etc. etc. etc.), or Canadian? Or all of those at once, even? Nalo Hopkinson got crap once for making the Toronto she writes about "too" full of POC (People of Color); I grew up in that exact same Toronto, man. It's hilarious, in context. Michael Rowe was a journalist, just like me; we both covered Don Hutchison's *Northern Frights* before getting published in it, which led to him publishing me in *Queer Fear*, and Brett Savory and Sandra Kasturi publishing both of us via ChiZine. David Demchuk wrote for the CBC before taking the world by storm with *The Bone Mother* and *Red X*. Charles de Lint spearheaded what we now call Urban Fantasy; Nancy Kilpatrick and Kelley Armstrong did the same for Paranormal Romance.

So here's the truth: We've been here the whole damn time, even when we were unaware of each other—but thank God, now we have the internet, so we can lift each other even higher, whenever we get the chance. Ai Jiang, Caitlin Marceau, Premee Mohammed, Ian Rogers, Richard Gavin, Simon Stranzas, and on and on and on. That big clot of all-Canadian dark just keeps on growing. I'm so happy to have been even vaguely part of making that happen, if I did.

EJG: Your novel *Experimental Film* won both the 2016 Shirley Jackson Award and the 2016 Sunburst Award, and was even identified by *Esquire* magazine as one of "The 50 Best Horror Books of All Time." The book is a remarkable blend of literary horror and weird fiction, and seems to draw many parallels to your own life, both personally and professionally. How close is protagonist Lois Cairns's life to your own?

The story is very grounded in reality, with a slow-reveal of otherworldly aspects beginning to occur, leading slowly and inexorably into a dark journey of tragedy and folklore. It's a complex narrative and as sharp in its social commentary as it is in its fictional evolution. There are a number of antagonists, both societal as well as supernatural, but the most prominent of these is the center point of Lois's research, the cruel Lady Midday who demands polite deference. What is the backstory to Lady Midday's conception and importance in this story? What does she represent?

GF: How close is Lois Cairns's life to my own? A lot. I tried to write *Experimental Film* for three years straight and kept failing. The breakthrough was realizing that I had to take all the crap I'd been feeling and channel it directly into the book to make it work … that I was the grit in question. I am mainly Lois, my son is mainly Clark, my husband is mainly Simon. And it helped. I like to think I'm nicer to my real mom on the regular, though, and that she's nicer to me.

And good question about the backstory and representation of Lady Midday. She is the creative muse—she strikes you with the spotlight of inspiration, gives you a vision and tells you to *do your work*, to sacrifice everything for it and be happy to, or act like you are. She's the sun and you're the lens, and if you make everything around you burst into fire in the service of your own gift, so what? *Blessed is the match, consumed in holy flame.* She masquerades as a fertility goddess, but she's actually the goddess of the harvest hour alone: She decides what gets cut down and what is allowed to flourish. She rejects the spoiled fruit, the bad seed, the imperfect, the useless; you will bury your "exceptional" children and your old people to feed her. She is ravenous, all-consuming. The gifts she gives are cruel. You cannot live forever in her gaze, but neither can you expect to. She is a splinter, a *little* god, a petty god. And therefore to reject her is easier than it would be to reject a *big* god, let alone the big-G God, if such a thing exists.

I think on some level that when I put Lady Midday together, when I wrote the Lady Midday fairytale that was *Experimental Film*'s true beginning, I was thinking of Frau Holle and Mrs. Gertrude and Baba Yaga, but all of those figures are ones you can bargain with, argue with; they'll eat you or they'll bless you, depending on whether they think you're smart or stupid. They can be monsters and fairy godmothers at the same time. But Lady Midday is something more narrow, like King Frost ("Are you warm, maiden? Are you warm?" "Very warm, King Frost."), or the Snow Queen. She's like the splinter in Kay's eye. You either agree with the way she sees things or you go blind.

EJG: Which of your writings would you most like to see adapted to film? (And what type of film would it do best on: silver nitrate, 35mm Technicolor, modern electronic, or other?)

GF: Oh boy. "The Sanguintalist" would make a great queer POC *Constantine*, and I'd want it done with a Riz Ahmed score, by a British director of South Asian heritage. Somebody wanted to do "Grave Goods," and *man* would I be on that train—I have a few casting ideas. *Experimental Film* could be done if you shot it as a mock-doc, moving between Safie and Lois's rough cut footage and the various Mrs. A. Whitcomb Macalla clips, maybe framing it with the denouement "explanation" and then undercutting it. There are a lot of filmmakers I'd give my left figurative nut to work with, especially if it required translating the stories from my culture to theirs—Park Chan-Wook, Timo Tjahanto, Kiyoshi Kurosawa. And I'm definitely not a nerd about production—any sort of filmmaking works, so long as it works within context. Where things fall down is when people shoot in digital and pretend it's film, etc.; digital's totally fine so long as that's the right medium for the story. See *Session 9*, amongst so many other things.

EJG: What are some of the trends you see (or foresee) in horror fiction (or literature, in general) today?

GF: I think the thing that's going to keep on happening is a sort of crossbreeding of narrative impulses. With me, you've seen a lot of focus on what I call "found footage on the page," which is really just a series of variations on the old-school Bram Stoker *Dracula* epistolary tale model; it's like making a collage from everything you can possibly hook into the story, telling it from every angle—inside and out, multiple-POV, multiple time-periods, fake fiction, fake non-fiction. It seems new, but people have been doing it here and there forever, from H.R. Wakefield to Esther Forbes. If you read widely, it all piles in on itself, and I love that. I love people who find something they've never seen before and imitate it; I love pastiche, creepypasta, dead tech, new tech. I love that the parameters of what we call horror keep on widening, because they *should*: Horror is the world's first literature. Horror is everything, or can be.

EJG: What's the best piece of advice someone has given you, and what's the worst piece of advice someone's given you?

GF: Keep writing, and "why don't you write something people actually *like*?"

EJG: What does the future hold for Gemma Files's writing career?

GF: My basic ambition has always been to write and get paid for writing until I die, which continues to seem pretty likely. That said, I'm really enjoying experimenting with visual art, and I'd still love to be involved in seeing my stuff adapted to film and/or television. So please get on that, somebody!

EJG: Thanks, Gemma! And yes, folks need to get on that pronto. I will not die happy unless I've seen a film adaptation of "The Emperor's Old Bones"!

(January 15, 2024)

Stories in Pieces: Found Footage Storytelling, or Writing Epistolary Narratives for the 21st Century (An Essay)

by Gemma Files

THE THESIS: IN A MEDIA-LITERATE AND -SATURATED age (such as ours), using as many different streams of information as required or possible to tell a story simply serves to make it seem more real, as does tricking the reader into thinking they're an active participant in the story as it unfolds—forcing them to study it, to follow the clues. Creating a maze only you have the key to, but one they can *find* the key to, with your help. Using text, subtext, and meta-text (text that comments on itself), each writer can decide on a strategy which makes sure readers get all the information they need in order to connect the dots along with you and feel as though they've helped "solve" the story by the time it ends, or at least stops.

The great part about epistolary/found footage storytelling is how surprisingly easy it can be to put a story like this together, much like building a collage, albeit one made out of images you yourself drew, then snipped apart for maximum impact. To tell a story from several different objective and subjective viewpoints, playing them off against each other to reveal a larger overall story, you can basically feel free to use every and/or any type of documentation you can think of, so long as it fits contextually: website entries, Wiki-data, emails, snail-mail letters, newspaper articles, media outlet posts, chat logs, blog or diary entries, comment threads, text messages, tweets, official documents, press releases, transcripts of podcasts and interviews, descriptions of visual/aural data—films, videos, .jpgs, .mpgs, sound-files, etc.

In Paul Tremblay's short story "Notes for 'The Barn in the Wild,'" for example—reprinted in his collection *Growing Things*—he replicates the text of a notebook in which our main perspective character is jotting down research, memoirish fragments, doodles, and various preliminary notes for an article he intends to write; as things become weirder, the protagonist finds notes he can't recall having made next to particular entries, and eventually whole pages in a degraded version of his own handwriting. But how different is this from, say, Bram Stoker's classic epistolary novel *Dracula*, stitched together as it is from diary entries, letters, clippings, telegrams, and various other effluvia produced by several different characters undergoing the same linked set of supernatural events? Or, for that matter, how different are either of these tales from Choderlos de Laclos's *Les Liaisons Dangereuses*, told as it is as a series of missives penned by two decadent aristocrats amusing themselves by manipulating and destroying various people they consider too naive or annoying to matter?

An argument could be made both that epistolary storytelling is one of the oldest types of fiction, and that the thing which makes it so innately fascinating, both as a practice and a form of reading matter, lies in exactly the same promise that attracts us to other sorts of metafiction, very much including found footage movies: The idea that by imitating the ways in which true-life events are documented (either during or after the fact), it allows writers to deliver on the most integral promise of storytelling itself, the impression of relating something that—while definitely *not* true—*could* be true.

Some of my favorite horror stories are epistolary narratives. "N" by Stephen King; the hypnagogic tales of podcaster Soren Narnia; "Pages from a Young Girl's Diary" by Robert Aickman; and on, and on, and on. At this point in my career, I've lost track of how many epistolary or semi-epistolary stories I've written, especially when you fold in the fact that any first-person narrative could be just as easily labelled epistolary—the text version of spoken testimony, or a piece of given evidence.

Like all classic hauntology (recordings, photos, film, etcetera produced during parapsychological inquiries), all found footage narratives—and, to some degree, Creepypasta—spin on the basic assumption that technology can render reality (or, at the least, our perception of reality) objective. "Pics or it didn't happen" becomes "video tells the truth, film lies," even when we all know that both film and video are equally easy to fake. But since we really all start out knowing better, because all stories are fiction, found footage is also inherently creepy from the get-go. Documentaries are assumed to be educational, trustworthy, yet every cut and splice acts as directorial POV, nudging you toward a foregone conclusion the filmmaker has already decided upon. The fun lies in the way that these narratives dole out the necessary information, making you feel you're putting the pieces together yourself.

Although we think of found footage as mainly a visual medium (the name suggests as much), these are tactics used in sensation/thriller/horror storytelling at least since the 1880s, throughout what the Victorians referred to as Sensation Literature. "The Call of Cthulhu," by H.P. Lovecraft, essentially consists of someone describing a bunch of material a friend of his found in a box he inherited from a dead relative and how he put these items together to suggest a larger, interconnecting story. *A Mirror for Witches*, by Esther Forbes, is formatted like a pamphlet from 1600s' Puritan New England chronicling the life and death of Doll Bilby, a woman accused of witchcraft. "Ghost Hunt," by H.R. Wakefield, is formatted as a taped monologue/radio broadcast delivered by a radio host who agrees to spend the night alone in a supposedly haunted house, climaxing with his own "live" suicide—it's also been adapted to "real" radio play format for various series, including *Suspense*.

The key, I believe, lies that most classic of Creepypasta lines: "Okay, so I know this sounds totally fake, but it's all true." By mixing and matching delivery systems, we create a net of suggestions which allow the reader to become a participant, essentially allowing them to trick themselves into believing in something they already know isn't real. It's just fiction to another level, but the suspension of disbelief required is even more gossamer-thin than usual and very easily punctuated, especially if you expand the story to include multiple POVs from very different character types.

On a purely practical level, the tricks of the trade may include:

INTERVIEWS (TRANSCRIBED)—taken in studio or in field. These play a lot like radio scripts, so the podcast model is a good thing to study; scripts or transcriptions of many podcasts can be found online. I'd recommend *The Black Tapes* podcast as a good place to start.

RESEARCH STRINGS—tracing how someone researches something, using much the same format as an Internet browser history list, but slightly more expanded. This might include cited quotations from books, articles, back-and-forth comments on articles, etc.

Official Documentation—site entries, Wiki-data, newspaper articles/media outlet posts, chat logs, comment threads, text messages, tweets, official documents, press releases, etc. Format is important, but not to the point of making yourself insane; find something to model your version after, then check it for errors once you're done with the first draft.

Monologues—blog/diary entries, letters, emails, transcribed livestreaming or live-Tweeting à la Seanan McGuire's short story, "#connollyhouse #weshouldntbehere". This last is an incredible challenge, especially since you have to run every section through Twitter to make sure it doesn't go over the character limit, but it's a wonderful way to make a story seem immediate, as if it's happening right before your eyes and your attention is part of the action. But on a slightly less technological tip, if you stick to physical documentation, you open yourself to being able to move freely between time-periods in a way most found footage won't allow, restricted as it is to eras after the motion picture camera was invented.

STRAIGHT DESCRIPTIONS OF VISUAL/AUDIO MEDIA—edited, unedited, collated, uncollated. Photos, film, and video clips or footage, .jpgs, .mpgs, sound-files … but as you go back further, you also find works organized around descriptions of statues, carvings (e.g., "The Last Sailing of the Henry Charles Morgan in Six Pieces of Scrimshaw (1841)" by A.C. Wise", mezzotints (e.g., "The Mezzotint" by M.R. James), daguerreotypes, Polaroids, and on and on, ad infinitum. Supposedly unchangeable things that change, or seem to change, according to their viewer ("Did you see what I saw?" "…what did you see?") are the very heart of Uncanny Valley territory, as "wrong" and dreadful as the idea of looking into a mirror and seeing someone else's face.

PROVENANCE—how did you get these documents? Where did you get these documents? Whose hands did they pass through? Have they been curated, overtly or inadvertently? Is anything missing, lost? What lens were the curators looking at this material through—what were their opinions/assumptions about their content? What are people choosing not to say/comment on, and why? (The lens of received wisdom can be fascinating to play with—i.e., in *A Mirror for Witches*, the pamphleteers "know" that Doll Bilby is a witch because it's commonly accepted fact, therefore everything they record "proves that she's a witch," whereas modern readers look at the same material and say "no, there's another possibility here—she might have just been driven crazy by everybody continually accusing her of witchcraft.") How can this information be reframed? How would you reframe it?

ANNOTATIONS/COMMENTARY—a wonderful example of this is Sarah Gailey's "STET", written as an article full of citations and editorial notes, all of which advance the overall story. Hard as hell to do, but possible! You can also put these in manually on the physical page as footnotes/endnotes or break to put the commentary in using a different font. See also Paul Tremblay's story "The Blog at the End of the World," *The Dionaea House* by Eric Heisserer, or "The Pine Arch Collection" by Michael Wehunt.

PERSPECTIVE—restricted or multiple? Single perspective is great for either total subjectivity or total objectivity, but multiple perspectives can be used to reveal information a single perspective might not have access to. It's also the difference between Adam L.G. Nevill's dereliction-type of story, "Hippocampus", in which literally nothing is explained (only described), and a version of the same scenario annotated/commented on by, say, experts in archaeology who might be able to explain where those weird mummies come from, or maritime disaster investigators who might be able to tell you what ship it was, who the crew were, etc. (Ask yourself if your story needs this sort of expansion.)

EMPATHY VS. SYMPATHY—one primary complaint about found footage is that the characters tend to be overly simple or inherently unsympathetic. This may be because of the inherent difference between an audience member being asked to put themselves in the position of a character and a reader being asked to make the same leap. The reader's perspective will always be more intimate. Another really important thing that too few people play with, however, is complicity—making the audience member/reader feel as though their outside-the-narrative perspective allows them to understand things the characters don't, or make connections before the characters have enough information to do so. In found footage narratives we are often unable to alter the story's trajectory ("one year later, their footage was found"), usually because it's already fixed directionally before we even begin our journey through it, yet this last aspect can allow us to feel a bit more in control. The most control, however, would be if the narrative was formatted like a game, with multiple potential twists and endings. (Very *Choose Your Own Adventure*—"if this, then this." Possible in prose? Certainly, though it's a challenge.)

EXPERIMENTATION—there's always a new sort of delivery system to play with. Think about police/military body-cams and private security surveillance tapes, drone footage, GPS and Fitbit readings uploaded automatically to the Cloud, downloading someone's voice-activated AI logs (Alexa recording a ghost's "voice" the same way a parrot might imitate the sound of someone being murdered). Anything and everything.

IMMEDIACY—is the story already done, or is it still happening? Is the narrator/editor part of it? Is the reader directly "threatened" by what goes on during the story they're reading?

Some other good things to keep in mind: Leave things to the imagination by considering framing—let stuff happen outside the frame of "the camera," as well as inside it. Noises in the dark count for a lot (which is why the invention of night-vision lenses has been a bad as well as a good thing for found footage). Maybe let the filming stop every once in a while, then rejoin your characters in progress, dropping readers back into the action without getting them up to speed. (The White Vault podcast uses an overall narrator to link sections of audio, thus skipping over—say—ten minutes of crawling through a tunnel, or eight hours of sleep.) Don't let the documentation be questioned (i.e. "why the hell are they still filming?"), perhaps by making at least one informational feed professional in nature—CCTV, news coverage, etc.

Switch perspectives to bring in new characters, which may in itself reframe the action (one of the best examples I've ever seen of this is in the novel *Security* by Gina Wohlsdorff, which is told entirely in CCTV feeds, one of which follows "the killer" doing things other characters can't see [and an overall narrator commenting on top of it, implying he may be the person employing said killer]). Part of the thrill of found footage is voyeurism, so use that. Also, bearing in mind frequent complaints that found footage horror protagonists often aren't "likeable," watching the horror unfold from the eyes of the person inflicting it could certainly both make for some uncomfortable reading and make us feel a lot more like rooting for the characters involved. And pay attention to dialogue, because when you reduce characters to speech and action, it's very easy for them to all sound the same. Try breaking straight description up with personal commentary/monologue, to give an insight into the people involved.

As with all sorts of fiction, the idea is to work out both the story you want to tell and how you want to tell it, with an eye toward efficiency as well as effect. But because this is horror, part of that is figuring out what you want to be "scary" about the situation outlined—how you're going to build up and then undermine a sense of reality. If your reader doesn't believe in the reality of the situation when things are going as they should, they're sure not going to care once things start going off the rails. For me, this is where it helps to insert an element of your own emotional reality wrapped inside a pellet of something so dramatic that anybody might be affected by it, but your process may be different.

Say we begin with a story idea about a woman whose wife has vanished. The outline of such a piece could involve three types of documentation: The first a newspaper article about the disappearance; the second a transcript of a wiretapped conversation (recorded by the police) between the woman and her brother-in-law; the third a series of entries from the woman's diary. The next step would involve figuring out a strategy of assemblage—how will you braid these streams of information together, and in what order? Where should you cut and/or paste? How will you find your narrative through-line, the information and events that move the plot forward most directly, let alone when and/or how to reveal these elements? Remember: At least one of your informational streams should always be from the POV of a main character, because character relationships are the primary mechanism that drives plot forward. We call this sort of stream the spine, and all the other streams orbit around it by necessity, interacting with it to produce a forward-moving story even if the story also contains information from the past (flashbacks told through older documentation), or information dropped in as a sort of sidebar (to elaborate on or inform the main text). Think of it like assembling a necklace out of three or more types of beads: Try to find, and make, a pattern.

I used to tell people that when you're writing something shorter than a novel, you sometimes have to make a choice between characterization and plot development... i.e., that the more detailed the plot is, the less deeply you can delve into the characters involved (and that it also helps to have fewer characters if you want to explore them more thoroughly). It's like the difference between inside action (thoughts, feelings, memories) and outside action (events, decisions, choices). But the fact is, even lightly characterized people mainly make decisions and choices because of their relationships with other people, and while you could call a lot of found footage narratives outside action-heavy, those relationships still need to exist in order to drive things along. It's the relationships that give us any type of sympathy with our protagonists, and plot without sympathy is just spectacle.

So how can you characterize people lightly and yet evoke sympathy? Well, it's a bit like knowing where to make the cuts when you're editing; in most cases, we skip the things that we think can be taken for granted. Sometimes it's stuff like: "How did this character get from here to there?" "Well, we can probably assume they used a vehicle of some sort, and that it took a certain amount of time. If it was a car, it might take minutes; if a bus or a truck, it might take hours. If a plane, it might take half a day, depending on where they're going." But sometimes it can also be stuff like: "If people are members of a family, we *begin* by assuming they probably love each other, which means they'll be afraid for each other if they're in danger and mourn for each other if something goes wrong. If one or more of them don't, that's worth covering, because that's the exception to the rule. It's worth going into, because it's different."

We assume that making an assumption (as the old phrase goes) makes an ass out of "u and me." But the fact is, a lot of the assumptions we make are about thing we generally understand. It's not a plot hole if someone tells somebody else they're coming to see them, and then a certain amount of narrative time later, they show up. You don't *have* to see the journey, unless something interesting happened along the way. And characterization can work a bit like that as well—if a mother hugs her son, that's pretty normal; if she tongue-kisses him and pulls him "offscreen," not so much. It makes us want to know more.

Figuring out your POV character and customizing one of the narrative streams—the spine—"for" them, if you haven't, is one of an epistolary narrative's most important challenges. Questions to ask in order to figure out the POV character might include: Who is telling each section of the story, and why? What parts are and are not most important? Is any of the testimony involved subjective? Then maybe the person whose POV reveals that fact is "the real" main character, the person we should be most invested in. (And BTW, it's possible to have more than one main character, though seldom more than three.)

Try to also think about indirect methods by which to achieve characterization—what objective facts we can learn about the characters through their choices and actions, and how those might be integral to the plot. For example: if a person has a family background of mental instability and becomes a completely logical atheist/doubter because of it, putting them up against something supernatural may cause them to make the wrong decisions simply because in order to make the right ones, they'd have to change their entire outlook on life. Some people can, but it costs them. Both sides of that struggle create drama. And think about the relationships that drive your POV character's intersection with the plot. Who do they love? Who do they hate? Why? What will they do or not do, because of these relationships?

Finally, there's a certain liminality which comes with a first-person perspective—do we believe what we're being told, or not? Did our narrator see what they think they saw? Were they wrong in their assumptions? Is there, in fact, an alternative explanation lurking between the lines, the images, the roster of evidence?

First off, let's define liminality, as a concept. Derived from the Latin word "limen," meaning, threshold, it was originally applied only to the transitional period or phase of a rite of passage—adolescence, for example, or being a student or trainee, engaged but not yet married, someone who isn't quite one thing or another, but exists in a literal state of flux. (Historically, the concept has also been applied to people undergoing FTM or MTF gender transition, or even people who identify as intersex, agender, asexual, or pansexual, as though these were negotiable states that haven't quite been "decided upon," but most people now understand that that's both inaccurate and potentially insulting. The term would, however, apply to those who identify as genderfluid.) In other words, state of liminality is one where the order of things has been suspended and is in flux, caught mid-transformation between fixed states.

The idea of liminality was first introduced into the field of anthropology in 1909 by Arnold Van Gennep, in his work *Les Rites de Passage*. Van Gennep described the rites of passage as having the following three-part structure: separation from the norm; a liminal period during which a new identity is decided upon; re-assimilation back into the norm. A person grieving a loss can be considered going through this pattern—she feels the loss, is inducted into a liminal transition period from grief to acceptance, then finally re-assimilates into society. It was not until the second half of the 20th Century, however—with the writings of Victor Turner, that the concept of liminality was explored fully. In *Liminality and Communitas*, Turner began by defining liminal individuals as "neither here nor there; they are betwixt and between the positions assigned and arrayed by law, custom, convention, and ceremony." But Turner gives hope by referring to "betwixt and between" through the concept of the "realm of pure possibility"—the idea that re-assimilation into a fixed state doesn't have to be the end of the story, and might not even be a happy one, if it is.

This reinterpretation leaves literal space for people—and narratives—which differ from the norm, horror stories very much amongst them.

Since my own inclinations are always to the dark, no matter what genre I'm dealing with, I tend to put things in horror terms. And luckily for me, horror is an inherently liminal genre, one whose central narrative convention as a whole may well be the realization—quick or slow, big or small, immediate or retroactive—that there is *something wrong*. This is one of the reasons why horror narratives so often tend to the conservative, or at least the predictable: because the discovery of wrongness means that there must have, originally, been a standard of innate rightness from which things can deviate. As such, you often feel you have only two choices: restore normalcy at the end of the narrative, or don't. Both choices can also seem utterly mundane, which is antithetical to the whole idea of horror and only half of the story when it comes to liminality.

So how do you get around this? In my opinion, first and foremost by playing with the delivery system: experimenting with or combining various narrative structures and methodologies, the mechanics of mood and character perspective—whatever it takes, according to the challenge. You look at the content of the story you want to tell and then shape the way you're going to tell it accordingly. Sometimes you go where it seems most natural to, and sometimes you try to set up tension by going in exactly the opposite direction. Or a combination of both.

In other words, if horror is inherently liminal, then so is found footage/epistolary storytelling. The two are made for each other. The single perspective of classic found footage can't possibly show you everything at once about a situation, so its very limitations help you to imagine what it can't show; expanded found footage/epistolary narrative allows for several perspectives (all equally limited on their own) crossing over and differing from each other, even contradicting each other, to create a composite, fragmentary picture of something impossible to describe directly.

Think of the central problem of adapting the works of HP Lovecraft, possibly the most liminal horror author of the whole classic horror canon. This quote from his story "The Unnamable" tells it best: "It was everywhere—a gelatin—a slime; a vapor;—yet it had shapes, a thousand shapes of horror beyond all memory. There were eyes—and a blemish. It was the pit—the maelstrom— the ultimate abomination. Carter, it was the unnamable!" Impossible to depict visually or through information-driven storytelling—but is it really? A thing that's all these things at once is liminal, wrong on every level . . . the only way you can come to it is through bits and snatches, at oblique angles, between the lines, liminally. By controlling not only what you choose to show, but what you choose not to.

I've often used the metaphor of an advent calendar—a series of doors covering a huge picture which we reveal part by part, by choosing what doors to open and in what order. Sometimes we do it from the bottom up or top down, from left to right or right to left; sometimes we open them in numerical order, and sometimes we just open them at random. It's up to us to figure out how best to do it, depending on our readers' powers of logic, analysis, and imagination. When we tell them that something's wrong, how long do we want it to take for them to figure out exactly what that is? Do we choose to do that in linear order, moving fairly smoothly from point to point on the curve, or in non-linear order, sending them in directions which turn out to be thematic or emotional sidebars, increasing a sense of dread and disturbance with giving any sort of narrative reward?

So on the one hand, telling stories of liminality not only produces but defines the sense of unreliability that horror depends on, and on the other, it's also a position of pure creative potential—things could literally go in any direction you want. It's a terrifying sense of freedom.

To get just a tad more technical, these might be the primary questions we ask ourselves when starting to rough out a horror idea:

What is wrong?

How do we find out it's wrong?

What's the fallout from that discovery?

Is it fixable?

(The horror impulse is to say "no," or "only at an almost equally intolerable price." Also, what value of "fix" are you willing to settle for?)

This wrongness might be something familiar rendered unfamiliar—indeed, especially when dealing with a short story, this is often the place most people tend to start, choosing to skip the world-building element entirely, given they don't have a lot of time and space to play with to begin with, and just assume that the world of the story mimics their/their reader's own. They begin with characters like them doing the sort of stuff they usually do, then introduce a very domestic sort of wrongness into the familiar scenario. But sometimes the wrongness involved is on a level far larger than that of a simple haunted object or person you think you know who suddenly isn't behaving "like [themself]." In some cases, horror comes out of the reader's own realization that a story's characters inhabit a completely different world than they themselves do, and don't necessarily even notice is inherently wrong, until said wrongness rebounds on them. Shirley Jackson's "The Lottery" is a prime example of this trope, as is Robert W. Chambers's "The Repairer of Reputations," which also happens to have a POV character who we only gradually realize is ass-crazy.

So perhaps, rather than wrongness, what we're actually looking to fashion here is more like... a sense of unreliability. What's going to turn out to be unreliable in your story? The narrator? The world? The frame? Objects in the foreground? In the background? Other characters? Your protagonist's memories? Space and time? Logical consequences for certain actions? (In a universe where ghosts, monsters, or dark gods exist, for example, evoking, mocking, or just finding yourself in proximity with these creatures would not be a very good idea. In one where the Christian God is just a psychological construct, on the other hand, relying on Him for help would be a very *bad* idea, or at least a pointless one.)

One of the most wonderful (and difficult) things to make unreliable is the reader's own assumptions about what sort of story this is. I mean, *you* know you're writing horror, but your reader doesn't have to—until it's too late. Kelly Link, whose stories often begin like sweet, slightly twee magic-realistic fables and end by punching your heart out, is very good at this sort of thematic switcheroo. So is Jonathan Carroll, who once had his main character get out of a tight spot by suddenly just ceasing to pretend she *wasn't* actually the anthropomorphic embodiment of Death. Both their stories often start in one place and end in another, merely through the simple yet integral trick of suddenly revealing their true nature/genre halfway through.

When I hit a block with my writing I tend to try a tense I've always avoided (I've done some surprisingly good work in second person present, i.e. "you are here, you do this," and I've secretly yearned to do something in the future, like Scott Edelman does with his brilliant story "What Will Come After"). Or I could do something all in dialogue, or get rid of dialogue entirely (Lovecraft!), which definitely works when it comes to framing something as an official document, or a diary entry, or a bunch of letters, articles, tweets. I might omit description, keep it all "offscreen," or go so deep into description almost nothing actually happens. I might tell the story backward, or non-linearly—or even interstitially, by mainly talking about the things *around* the most important part of your story, thus forcing readers to try and figure out what it is that my characters won't address directly. I might even try to avoid explanation, or even exposition—shuck the usual trappings, embrace the uncanny, the numinous, the self-contradictory.

What we learn from crossing horror with liminality—much like we learn from crossing horror with fiction in general—is that the norm is not the same for everybody; the default is not the same for everybody. It can't be. So go to the opposite of your default and see what the world looks like from there. See what becomes abnormal, "wrong," and horrifying *then*.

A Bibliography of English Language Fiction for Gemma Files

FOLLOWING IS A COMPLETE BIBLIOGRAPHY OF ENGLISH language fiction for Gemma Files through March, 2021. Not included are: foreign language translations, individual pieces of non-fiction, screenplays, or individual pieces of poetry.

Abbreviations Used:

(1) = indicates story's first publication. Omitted if story first published in author collection.

(c) = indicates the collection containing this story. If the collection is listed first, the story's first appearance was in this collection.

(r) = indicates this is a reprint appearance.

anth. = anthology

mag. = magazine

f.c. = fiction collection

ed. = edited

v. = magazine volume number

= magazine issue number

SHORT FICTION

"Always After Three"
>   (1) *Tales from the Lake: Volume 5* (anth., ed. Kenneth W. Cain): Crystal Lake Publishing, 2018.
>   (c) *In That Endlessness, Our End* (f.c.): Grimscribe Press, 2021.

"[Anasazi]"
>   (1) *A Mountain Walked* (anth., ed. S. T. Joshi): Centipede Press, 2014.

"Bear-Shirt" (var: "Bear Shirt")
>   (1) *Queer Fear: Gay Horror Fiction* (anth., ed. Michael Rowe): Arsenal Pulp Press, 2000.
>   (c) *Kissing Carrion* (f.c.): Prime Books/ Wildside Press, 2003.

"Black Box"
>   (1) *The Mammoth Book of Body Horror* (anth., ed. Paul Kane and Marie O'Regan): Robinson/ Running Press, 2012.
>   * also incl. in *We Will All Go Down Together: A Novel in Stories About the Five-Family Coven* (novel): ChiZine Publications, 2012.

"Black Bush"
>   (1) *Arcane* (anth., ed. Nathan Shumate): Cold Fusion Media, 2011.
>   (c) *Spectral Evidence* (f.c.): Trepidatio Publications, 2018.

"Blood Makes Noise"
>   (1) *Transversions* (mag, #11): Island Specialty Reports, 1999.
>   (r) *Creatures: Thirty Years of Monsters* (anth., ed. John Langan and Paul Tremblay): Prime Books, 2011.
>   (r) *Weird Fiction Review* (online media): weirdfictionreview.com, Mar. 2012.
>   (c) *Soaked in Light* (f.c.): Quantum Theology, 2000.
>   (c) *Kissing Carrion* (f.c.): Prime Books/ Wildside Press, 2003.

"Bottle of Smoke"
>   (1) *Demon Sex* (anth., ed. Amarantha Knight): Rhinoceros Fiction, 1997.
>   (c) *The Worm in Every Heart* (f.c.): Prime Books/ Wildside Press, 2004.

"Bulb"
>   (1) *New Fears 2* (anth., ed. Mark Morris): Titan Books, 2018.
>   (c) *In That Endlessness, Our End* (f.c.): Grimscribe Press, 2021.

"By the Mark"
>   *The Worm in Every Heart* (f.c.): Prime Books/ Wildside Press, 2004.
>   (r) *Bad Seeds: Evil Progeny* (anth., ed. Steve Berman): Prime Books, 2013.

"Caligarism"
>   (1) *The Madness of Dr. Caligari* (anth., ed. Joseph S. Pulver, Sr.): Fedogan & Bremer, 2016.

"Carmagnole"
>   (1) *The Willows: Complete Anthology* (anth., ed. Ben Thomas): Willows 2020, 2020.

"The Church in the Mountains"
>   (1) *Lost Films* (anth., ed. Max Booth, III and Lori Michelle): Perpetual Motion Machine Publishing, 2018.
>   (c) *In That Endlessness, Our End* (f.c.): Grimscribe Press, 2021.

"Come Closer"
>   (1) *Apostles of the Weird* (anth., ed. S.T. Joshi): PS Publishing, 2020.
>   (c) *In That Endlessness, Our End* (f.c.): Grimscribe Press, 2021.

"Copperplate"
>   (1) *The Kit (Compact Holiday)* (e-mag.): The Kit, a division of Toronto Star Newspapers Limited, Nov. 2017.

"Copy Degradation"
>   (1) *Black Static* (mag., #17): TTA Press, Jun./Jul. 2010.

"Crossing the River"

    (1) *Mighty Unclean* (anth., ed. Bill Breedlove): Dark Arts Books, 2009.

    (c) *Spectral Evidence* (f.c.): Trepidatio Publications, 2018.

"Cuckoo"

    In That Endlessness, Our End (f.c.): Grimscribe Press, 2021.

"Cut Frame"

    (1) *Final Cuts: New Tales of Hollywood Horror and Other Spectacles* (anth., ed. Ellen Datlow): Blumhouse Books, 2020.

    (c) *In That Endlessness, Our End* (f.c.): Grimscribe Press, 2021.

"Dead Bodies Possessed by Furious Motion"

    The Narrow World (f.c.): Quantum Theology, 2001.

    (c) *Kissing Carrion* (f.c.): Prime Books/ Wildside Press, 2003.

"The Diarist"

    (1) *Transversions* (mag, #7): Island Specialty Reports, 1997.

    (c) *Kissing Carrion* (f.c.): Prime Books/ Wildside Press, 2003.

"Distant Dark Places"

    (1) *Looming Low: Volume I* (anth., ed. Sam Cowan and Justin Steele): Dim Shores, 2017.

    (c) *In That Endlessness, Our End* (f.c.): Grimscribe Press, 2021.

"Down In It"

    (1) *Horror Carousel* (mag (fan-zine), #5): Horror Carousel, Spring 2007.

"Drawn Up From Deep Places"

    (1) *Beneath Ceaseless Skies* (e-mag., #159): Beneath Ceaseless Skies, Oct. 2014.

    (r) *The Best of Beneath Ceaseless Skies Online Magazine, Year Seven* (anth., ed. Scott H. Andrews): Firkin Press, 2016.

    (c) *Drawn Up from Deep Places* (f.c.): Trepidatio Publications, 2018.

"Drone"

    (1) *Not One of Us* (mag (fan-zine), #39): not-one-of-us.pub, Apr. 2008.

"each thing i show you is a piece of my death" (with Stephen J. Barringer)
> (1) *Clockwork Phoenix 2: More Tales of Beauty and Strangeness* (anth., ed. Mike Allen): Norilana Books, 2009.
> (r) *Apex Magazine* (e-mag., #16): Apex Publications, Sep. 2010.
> (r) *The Best Horror of the Year: Volume Two* (anth., ed. Ellen Datlow): Night Shade Books, 2010.
> (r) *The Cutting Room* (anth., ed. Ellen Datlow): Tachyon Publications, 2014.

"The Emperor's Old Bones"
> (1) *Northern Frights 5* (anth., ed. Don Hutchison): Mosaic Press, 1999.
> (r) *The Year's Best Fantasy and Horror: Thirteenth Annual Collection* (anth., ed. Ellen Datlow and Terri Windling): St. Martin's Griffin, 2000.
> (r) *The Mammoth Book of Best New Horror, Vol. 11* (anth., ed. Stephen Jones): Carroll & Graf, 2000.
> (r) *Wild Things Live There: The Best of Northern Frights* (anth., ed. Don Hutchison): Mosaic Press, 2001.
> (r) *The Humanity of Monsters* (anth., ed. Michael Matheson): ChiZine Publications, 2015.
> (r) *Nightmare Magazine* (online media): nightmare-mag.com, Nov. 2015.
> (c) *Soaked in Light* (f.c.): Quantum Theology, 2000.
> (c) *The Worm in Every Heart* (f.c.): Prime Books/ Wildside Press, 2004.

"Every Angel" (chapbook)
> (1) Kelp Queen Press, 2006.
> (r) *Innsmouth Magazine* (mag, #14): Innsmouth Free Press, Nov. 2013.
> (r) *Fright Into Flight* (anth., ed. Amber Fallon): Word Horde, 2018.

"Every Hole in the Earth We Will Claim as Our Own"
> (1) *Dreams from the Witch House: Female Voices of Lovecraftian Horror* (anth., ed. Lynne Jamneck): Dark Regions Press, 2016.

"A **F**east For Dust"
> (1) *Beneath Ceaseless Skies* (e-mag., #132): Beneath Ceaseless Skies, Oct. 2013.
>
> (r) *The Best of Beneath Ceaseless Skies Online Magazine, Year Six* (anth., ed. Scott H. Andrews): Firkin Press, 2015.
>
> (r) *Ceaseless West: Weird Western Stories from Beneath Ceaseless Skies Online Magazine* (anth., ed. Scott H. Andrews): Firkin Press, 2015.
>
> (r) *Lost Trails: Forgotten Tales of the Weird West: Volume 2* (anth., ed. Cynthia Ward): WolfSinger Publications, 2016.
>
> (c) *Drawn Up from Deep Places* (f.c.): Trepidatio Publications, 2018.

"The **F**ilthy Creation of Frankenstein"
> (1) *Behold the Undead of Dracula: Lurid Tales of Cinematic Gothic Horror* (anth., ed. Jonathan Raab): Muzzleland Press, 2019.

"**F**in De Siècle"
> (1) *Dark Faith: Invocations* (anth., ed. Maurice Broaddus and Jerry Gordon): Apex Publications, 2012.
>
> (r) *Imaginarium 2013: The Best Canadian Speculative Writing* (anth., ed. Sandra Kasturi and Samantha Beiko): ChiZine Publications, 2013.

"**F**lare"
> (1) *Dangerous Women* (anth., ed. S.G. Johnson): Obelesk Books, 1994.
>
> (c) *The Worm in Every Heart* (f.c.): Prime Books/Wildside Press, 2004.

"**F**ly-by-Night"
> (1) *The Vampire's Crypt* (mag, #8): Margaret L. Carter, Fall 1993.
>
> (c) *The Worm in Every Heart* (f.c.): Prime Books/ Wildside Press, 2004.

"**F**olly"
> (1) *2001 World Fantasy Convention: "Je me souviens… "* (anth., ed. Matthew Frederick, Margaret Grady, Nancy Kilpatrick, and Hugues Leblanc): World Fantasy Convention, 2001.
>
> (c) *Kissing Carrion* (f.c.): Prime Books/ Wildside Press, 2003.

"Furious Angels"

(1) *We Will All Go Down Together: A Novel in Stories About the Five-Family Coven* (story within the novel): ChiZine Publications, 2012.

"Gabbeh"

(1) *World Fantasy Convention Toronto 2012: Northern Gothic and Urban Fantasy* (anth., ed. Barbara Roden and Christopher Roden): World Fantasy Convention, 2012.

(r) *Postscripts to Darkness* (online media): pstdarkness.com, Feb. 2018.

"Gaze"

(1) *The Doll Collection* (anth., ed. Ellen Datlow): Tor, 2015.

"Grave Goods"

(1) *Autumn Cthulhu* (anth., ed. Mike Davis): Lovecraft eZine Press, 2016.

(r) *The Year's Best Dark Fantasy and Horror: 2017 Edition* (anth., ed. Paula Guran): Prime Books, 2017.

(r) *The Best Horror of the Year: Volume Nine* (anth., ed. Ellen Datlow): Night Shade Books, 2017.

(r) *The Best of the Best Horror of the Year: 10 Years of Essential Short Horror Fiction* (anth., ed. Ellen Datlow): Night Shade Books, 2018.

(r) *Nightmare Magazine* (online media): nightmare-mag.com, Oct. 2019.

"The Guided Tour"

(1) *The Vampire's Crypt* (mag, #13): Margaret L. Carter, Spring 1996.

"Guising"

(1) *October Dreams II: A Celebration of Halloween* (anth., ed. Richard Chizmar and Robert Morrish): Cemetery Dance Publications, 2015.

(c) *Spectral Evidence* (f.c.): Trepidatio Publications, 2018.

(c) *Exploring Dark Short Fiction #7: A Primer to Gemma Files* (f.c., ed. Eric J. Guignard): Dark Moon Books, 2025.

"Hairwork"

(1) *She Walks in Shadows* (anth., ed. Silvia Moreno-Garcia and Paula R. Stiles): Innsmouth Free Press, 2015.

(r) *rereleased as: *Cthulhu's Daughters: Stories of Lovecraftian Horror* (anth., ed. Silvia Moreno-Garcia and Paula R. Stiles): Prime Books, 2016.

(r) *The Year's Best Dark Fantasy and Horror: 2016 Edition* (anth., ed. Paula Guran): Prime Books, 2016.

(r) *The Dark* (e-mag., #19): Prime Books, Dec. 2016.

(r) *The Mammoth Book of Best New Horror, Vol. 27* (anth., ed. Stephen Jones): Drugstore Indian Press, 2017.

"Halloo"

(1) *Phantoms* (anth., ed. Marie O'Regan): Titan Books, 2018.

(c) *In That Endlessness, Our End* (f.c.): Grimscribe Press, 2021.

"The Harrow"

(1) *The Children of Old Leech: A Tribute to the Carnivorous Cosmos of Laird Barron* (anth., ed. Ross E. Lockhart and Justin Steele): Word Horde, 2014.

(r) *Chthonic: Weird Tales of Inner Earth* (anth., ed. Scott R. Jones): Martian Migraine Press, 2018.

"Heart-Dust"

(1) *Horror Carousel* (mag (fan-zine), #4): Horror Carousel, Spring 2006.

"Heart's Hole"

(1) *In the Dark: Stories from the Supernatural* (anth., ed. Myna Wallin and Halli Villegas): Tightrope Books, 2006.

* also incl. in *We Will All Go Down Together: A Novel in Stories About the Five-Family Coven* (novel): ChiZine Publications, 2012.

"Hell Friend"

(1) *Clockwork Phoenix 3: New Tales of Beauty and Strangeness* (anth., ed. Mike Allen): Norilana Books, 2010.

(c) *Drawn Up from Deep Places* (f.c.): Trepidatio Publications, 2018.

"Helpless"
> (1) *We Will All Go Down Together: A Novel in Stories About the Five-Family Coven* (story within the novel): ChiZine Publications, 2012.

"Hexmas: A Hexslinger Tale"
> (1) (chapbook): ChiZine Publications, 2014.
> (c) *The Hexslinger Omnibus* (omnibus) (f.c.): ChiZine Publications, 2012.

"Hidebound"
> (1) *Transversions* (mag, #5): Island Specialty Reports, 1997.
> (c) *Kissing Carrion* (f.c.): Prime Books/ Wildside Press, 2003.

"His Face, All Red"
> (1) *Stamps, Vamps & Tramps* (anth., ed. Shannon Robinson): Evil Girlfriend Media, 2014.
> (c) *Spectral Evidence* (f.c.): Trepidatio Publications, 2018.

"History's Crust"
> (1) *We Will All Go Down Together: A Novel in Stories About the Five-Family Coven* (story within the novel): ChiZine Publications, 2012.

"Homebody"
> (1) *Chilling Tales Two: In Words, Alas, Drown I* (anth., ed. Michael Kelly): Edge Science Fiction and Fantasy Publishing, 2013.

"Imaginary Beauties" (var: "Imaginary Beauties: A Lurid Melodrama") (chapbook)
> (1) Kelp Queen Press, 2008.
> (r) *Daughters of Frankenstein: Lesbian Mad Scientists* (anth., ed. Steve Berman): Lethe Press, 2015.
> (c) *Spectral Evidence* (f.c.): Trepidatio Publications, 2018.

"In Hell, an Eye"
> (1) *Eulogies III* (anth., ed. Christopher Jones, Nanci Kalanta, and Tony Tremblay): HW Press, 2015.

"In Scarlet Town (Today): A Hexslinger Tale"
>   (1) (chapbook): ChiZine Publications, 2014.
>   (c) *The Hexslinger Omnibus* (omnibus) (f.c.): ChiZine Publications, 2012.

"In the Poor Girl Taken by Surprise"
>   *The Worm in Every Heart* (f.c.): Prime Books/ Wildside Press, 2004.
>   (r) *The Mammoth Book of Monsters* (anth., ed. Stephen Jones): Carroll & Graf/ Robinson, 2007.
>   (r) *Pseudopod* (podcast/ audio, #257): Escape Artists, Inc., Nov. 2011.
>   (c) *Exploring Dark Short Fiction #7: A Primer to Gemma Files* (f.c., ed. Eric J. Guignard): Dark Moon Books, 2025.

"The Jacaranda Smile"
>   (1) *Apparitions* (anth., ed. Michael Kelly): Undertow Publications, 2009.
>   (r) *The Year's Best Dark Fantasy and Horror: 2010 Edition* (anth., ed. Paula Guran): Prime Books, 2010.

"Jack-Knife: A Melodrama Inspired from Life in Fourteen Vocal Tableaux, Best Heard in a Dark Room, the Doors Locked"
>   (1) *Shivers IV* (anth., ed. Richard Chizmar): Cemetery Dance Publications, 2006.
>   (c) *Drawn Up from Deep Places* (f.c.): Trepidatio Publications, 2018.

"Job 37"
>   (1) *Dark Terrors 6: The Gollancz Book of Horror* (anth., ed. Stephen Jones and David Sutton): Gollancz/ Orion, 2002.
>   (c) *Kissing Carrion* (f.c.): Prime Books/ Wildside Press, 2003.

"Keepsake"
>   (1) *Palace Corbie* (mag, #7): Merrimack Books, Apr. 1997.
>   (r) *The Best of Palace Corbie* (anth., ed. Wayne Edwards): Stone Dragon Press, 1999.
>   (c) *Soaked in Light* (f.c.): Quantum Theology, 2000.
>   (c) *Kissing Carrion* (f.c.): Prime Books/ Wildside Press, 2003.

"The **K**indly Ones"
> *The Worm in Every Heart* (f.c.): Prime Books/ Wildside Press, 2004.

"**K**issing Carrion"
> *Kissing Carrion* (f.c.): Prime Books/ Wildside Press, 2003.
> (r) *The Mammoth Book of Best New Horror, Vol. 15* (anth., ed. Stephen Jones): Carroll & Graf, 2004.
> (r) *Dead North: The Exile Book of Canadian Zombie Fiction* (anth., ed. Silvia Moreno-Garcia): Exile Editions, 2013.

"**L**agan"
> (1) *Unspeakable Horror 2: Abominations of Desire* (anth., ed. Vince A. Liaguno): Evil Jester Press, 2017.
> (r) *The Mammoth Book of Best New Horror, Vol. 29* (anth., ed. Stephen Jones): Drugstore Indian Press, 2019.

"The **L**and Beyond the Forest"
> (1) *The Vampire's Crypt* (mag, #10): Margaret L. Carter, Fall 1994.
> (c) *The Worm in Every Heart* (f.c.): Prime Books/ Wildside Press, 2004.

"**L**andscape with Maps & Legends: Dead Voices on Air"
> (1) *Suspect Thoughts: A Journal of Subversive Writing* (e-mag., #17): Suspect Thoughts Press, (ca.) 2010.
> * also incl. in *We Will All Go Down Together: A Novel in Stories About the Five-Family Coven* (novel): ChiZine Publications, 2012.

"**L**ike a Bowl of Fire: A Hexslinger Tale"
> (1) (chapbook): ChiZine Publications, 2014.
> (c) *The Hexslinger Omnibus* (omnibus) (f.c.): ChiZine Publications, 2012.

"**L**ittle Ease"
> (1) *Children of Lovecraft* (anth., ed. Ellen Datlow): Dark Horse Books, 2016.

"**L**ook **U**p"
> (1) *The Weird Fiction Review #10* (anth., ed. John Pelan): Centipede Press, 2019.

(c) *In That Endlessness, Our End* (f.c.): Grimscribe Press, 2021.

"Marya Nox"

(1) *Lovecraft Unbound: Twenty Stories* (anth., ed. Ellen Datlow): Dark Horse Books, 2009.

"Mouthful of Pins"

(1) *White Wall Review* (mag, #15): Ryerson Literary Society, 1990.

(r) *Northern Frights 2* (anth., ed. Don Hutchison): Mosaic Press, 1994.

(c) *Kissing Carrion* (f.c.): Prime Books/ Wildside Press, 2003.

"Nanny Grey"

(1) *Magic: An Anthology of the Esoteric and Arcane* (anth., ed. Jonathan Oliver): Solaris, 2012.

(r) *The Best Horror of the Year: Volume Five* (anth., ed. Ellen Datlow): Night Shade Books, 2013.

(r) *Nightmare Magazine* (online media): nightmare-mag.com, Dec. 2018.

"The Narrow World"

The Narrow World (f.c.): Quantum Theology, 2001.

(r) *Queer Fear II* (anth., ed. Michael Rowe): Arsenal Pulp Press, 2002.

(c) *The Worm in Every Heart* (f.c.): Prime Books/ Wildside Press, 2004.

* also incl. in *We Will All Go Down Together: A Novel in Stories About the Five-Family Coven* (novel): ChiZine Publications, 2012.

"Night-Bird"

(1) *Aghast* (mag, #1): Kraken Press, Oct. 2016.

"Nigredo"

The Worm in Every Heart (f.c.): Prime Books/ Wildside Press, 2004.

"**N**o Darkness But Ours"
>   (1) *Twilight Showcase* (e-mag., #29): Strange Concepts Ltd. (Gary W. Conner), Nov. 2001–Jan. 2002.
>   (c) *Kissing Carrion* (f.c.): Prime Books/ Wildside Press, 2003.

"**O**ne in the Morning and One at Night"
>   (1) *Three-Lobed Burning Eye* (e-mag., #23): Three-Lobed Burning Eye, May 2013.
>   (r) *Three-Lobed Burning Eye Volume VI* (anth., ed. Andrew S. Fuller): Legion Press, 2020.

"**O**ubliette"
>   (1) *The Grimscribe's Puppets: A Tribute to Thomas Ligotti* (anth., ed. Joseph S. Pulver, Sr.): Miskatonic River Press, 2013.
>   (r) *Imaginarium 3: The Best Canadian Speculative Writing* (anth., ed. Sandra Kasturi and Helen Marshall): ChiZine Publications, 2015.

"**P**en Umbra"
>   (1) *Thrillers 2* (anth., ed. Robert Morrish): Cemetery Dance Publications, 2004.
>   * also incl. in *We Will All Go Down Together: A Novel in Stories About the Five-Family Coven* (novel): ChiZine Publications, 2012.

"**P**retend That We're Dead"
>   (1) *Three-Lobed Burning Eye* (e-mag., #7): Three-Lobed Burning Eye, Oct. 2000.
>   (r) *Three-Lobed Burning Eye Annual II* (anth., ed. Andrew S. Fuller): Legion Press, 2004.
>   (c) *The Narrow World* (f.c.): Quantum Theology, 2001.
>   (c) *Kissing Carrion* (f.c.): Prime Books/ Wildside Press, 2003.

"The **P**uppet Motel"
>   (1) *Echoes* (anth., ed. Ellen Datlow): Saga Press, 2019.
>   (c) *In That Endlessness, Our End* (f.c.): Grimscribe Press, 2021.

"The **R**ed Girl of Chatouye" (with Michael Bukowski)

    (1) *Yog-Blogsoth* (online media): http://yog-blogsoth.blogspot.com, May 2014.

    (r) *Illustro Obscurum Book Of One Thousand Forms I* (f.c. of Michael Bukowski): Seventh Church of the Illuminator Press, 2015.

"**R**ed Words"

    (1) *Sisterhood: Dark Tales and Secret Histories* (anth., ed. Nate Pedersen): Chaosium Inc., 2018.

"**R**ing of Fire"

    (1) *Palace Corbie* (mag, #6): Merrimack Books, Dec. 1995.

    (r) *Mighty Unclean* (anth., ed. Bill Breedlove): Dark Arts Books, 2009.

    (c) *Soaked in Light* (f.c.): Quantum Theology, 2000.

    (c) *The Worm in Every Heart* (f.c.): Prime Books/ Wildside Press, 2004.

"**R**ose-Sick"

    (1) *Seductive Spectres* (anth., ed. Amarantha Knight): Rhinoceros Fiction, 1996.

    (r) *Haunted are These Houses* (anth., ed. Eddie Generous): Unnerving, 2018.

    (c) *Kissing Carrion* (f.c.): Prime Books/ Wildside Press, 2003.

"The **S**alt Wedding"

    (1) *Kaleidotrope* (e-mag): Kaleidotrope (Fred Coppersmith), Winter, 2015.

    (c) *Drawn Up from Deep Places* (f.c.): Trepidatio Publications, 2018.

"**S**atan's Jewel Crown"

    (1) *Dark Discoveries* (mag., #26): JournalStone, Winter, 2014.

    (c) *Drawn Up from Deep Places* (f.c.): Trepidatio Publications, 2018.

"**S**een"

    The Narrow World (f.c.): Quantum Theology, 2001.

    (c) *Kissing Carrion* (f.c.): Prime Books/ Wildside Press, 2003.

"Sent Down"

(1) *Terror Tales 2* (anth., ed. John B. Ford and Paul Kane): Rainfall Books, 2004.

(c) *The Worm in Every Heart* (f.c.): Prime Books/ Wildside Press, 2004.

"The Shrines"

(1) *Chilling Tales: Evil Did I Dwell; Lewd Did I Live* (anth., ed. Mike Kelly): Edge Science Fiction and Fantasy Publishing, 2011.

"Signal to Noise"

(1) *The Chiaroscuro* (online media, #47): chizine.com, Apr.–Jun. 2011.

(r) *Imaginarium 2012: The Best Canadian Speculative Writing* (anth., ed. Sandra Kasturi and Halli Villegas): ChiZine Publications, 2012.

(r) *Apex Magazine* (e-mag., #78): Apex Publications, Nov. 2015.

"A Single Shadow Make"

(1) *Techno Myths* (anth., ed. S.G. Johnson): Obelesk Books, 1994.

(c) *The Worm in Every Heart* (f.c.): Prime Books/ Wildside Press, 2004.

"Skeleton Bitch"

(1) *Palace Corbie* (mag, #5): Merrimack Books, Jan. 1994.

(c) *Kissing Carrion* (f.c.): Prime Books/ Wildside Press, 2003.

"Skin City"

(1) *A Crimson Kind of Evil* (anth., ed. S.G. Johnson): Obelesk Books, 1994.

(r) *Grue Magazine* (mag, #16): Hell's Kitchen Productions, Summer 1994.

(c) *Kissing Carrion* (f.c.): Prime Books/ Wildside Press, 2003.

"Sleep Hygiene"

(1) *Nightmare's Realm: New Tales of the Weird and Fantastic* (anth., ed. S. T. Joshi): Dark Regions Press, 2017.

(c) *In That Endlessness, Our End* (f.c.): Grimscribe Press, 2021.

"Slick Black Bones and Soft Black Stars"
    (1) *A Season in Carcosa* (anth., ed. Joseph S. Pulver, Sr.): Miskatonic River Press, 2012.
    (r) *The Mammoth Book of Best New Horror, Vol. 24* (anth., ed. Stephen Jones): Running Press, 2013.
    (c) *Exploring Dark Short Fiction #7: A Primer to Gemma Files* (f.c., ed. Eric J. Guignard): Dark Moon Books, 2025.

"Some Kind of Light Shines from Your Face"
    (1) *Gutshot: Weird West Stories* (anth., ed. Conrad Williams): PS Publishing, 2011.
    (r) *The Mammoth Book of Best New Horror, Vol. 23* (anth., ed. Stephen Jones): Running Press, 2012.

"Somnophilia"
    (1) *NASTY: Fetish Fights Back: An Erotic Short Story Collection* (anth., ed. Anna Yeatts and Chris Phillips): Anna Yeatts, 2017.

"Sown from Salt"
    (1) *The Harrow* (online media, vol. 11, #12): theharrow.com, 2008.
    (r) *Tales to Terrify* (podcast/ audio, #6): talestoterrify.com, Feb. 2012.
    (r) *Lost Trails: Forgotten Tales of the Weird West: Volume 1* (anth., ed. Cynthia Ward): WolfSinger Publications, 2015.
    (c) *Drawn Up from Deep Places* (f.c.): Trepidatio Publications, 2018.
    (c) *Exploring Dark Short Fiction #7: A Primer to Gemma Files* (f.c., ed. Eric J. Guignard): Dark Moon Books, 2025.

"Spectral Evidence"
    (1) *The Chiaroscuro* (online media, #30): chizine.com, Oct. 2006.
    (r) *Hauntings* (anth., ed. Ellen Datlow): Tachyon Publications, 2013.
    (r) *Nightmares: A New Decade of Modern Horror* (anth., ed. Ellen Datlow): Tachyon Publications, 2016.
    (c) *Spectral Evidence* (f.c.): Trepidatio Publications, 2018.

"The Speed of Pain"

> (1) *Mighty Unclean* (anth., ed. Bill Breedlove): Dark Arts Books, 2009.
>
> (c) *Spectral Evidence* (f.c.): Trepidatio Publications, 2018.

"Strange Weight"

> (1) *We Will All Go Down Together: A Novel in Stories About the Five-Family Coven* (story within the novel): ChiZine Publications, 2012.

"The Testament of Carnamagos"

> (1) *The Starry Wisdom Library: The Catalogue of the Greatest Occult Book Auction of All Time* (anth., ed. Nate Pedersen): PS Publishing, 2014.

"That Place"

> (1) *Letters to Lovecraft: Eighteen Whispers to the Darkness* (anth., ed. Jesse Bullington): Stone Skin Press, 2014.

"The Thin Places"

> (1) *The National Post* (newspaper: "Halloween Special Issue"): Oct., 27, 2015.
>
> (r) *Weird Dream Society: An Anthology of the Possible & Unsubstantiated in Support of RAICES* (anth., ed. Julie C. Day): Reckoning Press, 2020.

"Thin Cold Hands"

> (1) *LampLight* (mag., v.6, #4): Apokrupha, Jun. 2018.
>
> (r) *The Best Horror of the Year: Volume Eleven* (anth., ed. Ellen Datlow): Night Shade Books, 2019.
>
> (c) *In That Endlessness, Our End* (f.c.): Grimscribe Press, 2021.

"This Is How It Goes"

> (1) *Other Voices, Other Tombs* (anth., ed. John Brhel and Joe Sullivan): Cemetery Gates Media, 2019.
>
> (c) *In That Endlessness, Our End* (f.c.): Grimscribe Press, 2021.

"This Is Not For You"

> (1) *Nightmare Magazine* (mag., #25): Nightmare Magazine, Oct. 2014 (*normally an online mag; special print issue as *Women Destroy Horror!*).

> (r) *The Best Horror of the Year: Volume Seven* (anth., ed. Ellen Datlow): Night Shade Books, 2015.

"Torch Song"

> (1) *Transversions* (mag, #8/9): Island Specialty Reports, 1998.

> (c) *Kissing Carrion* (f.c.): Prime Books/ Wildside Press, 2003.

"Trap-Weed"

> (1) *Clockwork Phoenix 4* (anth., ed. Mike Allen): Mythic Delirium Books, 2013.

> (r) *Imaginarium 3: The Best Canadian Speculative Writing* (anth., ed. Sandra Kasturi and Helen Marshall): ChiZine Publications, 2015.

> (c) *Drawn Up from Deep Places* (f.c.): Trepidatio Publications, 2018.

"Twilight State"

> (1) *Genius Loci: Tales of the Spirit of Place* (anth., ed. Jaym Gates): Ragnarok Publications, 2016.

"Two Captains"

> (1) *Beneath Ceaseless Skies* (e-mag., #125): Beneath Ceaseless Skies, Jul. 2013.

> (r) *The Best of Beneath Ceaseless Skies Online Magazine, Year Five* (anth., ed. Scott H. Andrews): Firkin Press, 2014.

> (c) *Drawn Up from Deep Places* (f.c.): Trepidatio Publications, 2018.

"The Underneath"

> (1) *Shroud: The Quarterly Journal of Dark Fiction and Art* (mag, #8): Shroud Publishing, May 2010.

"Venio"

> (1) *Vastarien* (mag, v.2, #1): Grimscribe Press, Spring 2019.

> (r) *Pseudopod* (podcast/ audio, #673): Escape Artists, Inc., Nov. 2019.

(c) *In That Endlessness, Our End* (f.c.): Grimscribe Press, 2021.

(c) *Exploring Dark Short Fiction #7: A Primer to Gemma Files* (f.c., ed. Eric J. Guignard): Dark Moon Books, 2025.

"Villa Locusta"

(1) *The Harrow* (online media, vol. 10, #1): theharrow.com, 2007.

(c) *Drawn Up from Deep Places* (f.c.): Trepidatio Publications, 2018.

"What You See (When the Lights Are Out)"

(1) *Strangers Among Us: Tales of the Underdogs and Outcasts* (anth., ed. Susan Forest and Lucas K. Law): Laksa Media, 2016.

"When I'm Armouring My Belly"

(1) *Evolve: Vampire Stories of the New Undead* (anth., ed. Nancy Kilpatrick): Edge Science Fiction and Fantasy Publishing, 2010.

(c) *Spectral Evidence* (f.c.): Trepidatio Publications, 2018.

"A Wish From a Bone"

(1) *Fearful Symmetries* (anth., ed. Ellen Datlow): ChiZine Publications, 2014.

(r) *The Year's Best Dark Fantasy and Horror: 2015 Edition* (anth., ed. Paula Guran): Prime Books, 2015.

(r) *The Monstrous* (anth., ed. Ellen Datlow): Tachyon Publications, 2015.

(r) *Imaginarium 4: The Best Canadian Speculative Writing* (anth., ed. Sandra Kasturi and Jerome Stueart): ChiZine Publications, 2016.

(c) *Spectral Evidence* (f.c.): Trepidatio Publications, 2018.

"Words Written Backwards" (chapbook)

(1) Burning Effigy Press, 2007.

* also incl. in *We Will All Go Down Together: A Novel in Stories About the Five-Family Coven* (novel): ChiZine Publications, 2012.

"Worm Moon"

(1) *Pluto in Furs: Tales of Diseased Desires and Seductive Horrors* (anth., ed. Scott Dwyer): Plutonian Press, 2019.

(c) *In That Endlessness, Our End* (f.c.): Grimscribe Press, 2021.

"Year Zero"
>   (1) *The Mammoth Book of Vampire Stories by Women* (anth., ed. Stephen Jones): Carroll & Graf/ Robinson, 2001.
>   (c) *The Worm in Every Heart* (f.c.): Prime Books/ Wildside Press, 2004.

"Yol"
>   (1) *Exploring Dark Short Fiction #7: A Primer to Gemma Files* (f.c., ed. Eric J. Guignard): Dark Moon Books, 2025.

NOVELS, CHAPBOOKS, and OTHER STAND-ALONE WORKS

A Book of Tongues: Volume One of the Hexslinger Series (novel): ChiZine Publications, 2010.

Coffle (novella): Dim Shores, 2017.

Every Angel (chapbook): Kelp Queen Press, 2006.

Experimental Film (novel): ChiZine Publications, 2015.

The Hexslinger Omnibus (omnibus): ChiZine Publications, 2012 (ebook only) (collects three published *Hexslinger* novels plus additional tie-in short stories).

Imaginary Beauties (var: Imaginary Beauties: A Lurid Melodrama (chapbook): Kelp Queen Press, 2006.

A Rope of Thorns: Volume Two of the Hexslinger Series (novel): ChiZine Publications, 2011.

A Tree of Bones: Volume Three of the Hexslinger Series (novel): ChiZine Publications, 2012.

We Will All Go Down Together: A Novel in Stories About the Five-Family Coven (novel): ChiZine Publications, 2012.

Words Written Backwards (chapbook): Burning Effigy Press, 2007.

COLLECTIONS

Drawn Up from Deep Places (fiction collection): Trepidatio Publications, 2018.

Exploring Dark Short Fiction #7: A Primer to Gemma Files (fiction collection, ed. Eric J. Guignard): Dark Moon Books, 2025.

In That Endlessness, Our End (fiction collection): Grimscribe Press, 2021.

Kissing Carrion (fiction collection): Prime Books/ Wildside Press, 2003.

The Narrow World (limited edition, mini fiction collection): Quantum Theology, 2001.

Soaked in Light (limited edition, mini fiction collection): Quantum Theology, 2000.

Spectral Evidence (fiction collection): Trepidatio Publications, 2018.

The Worm in Every Heart (fiction collection): Prime Books/ Wildside Press, 2004.

COLLECTIONS OF POETRY (CHAPBOOKS)

Bent Under Night (poetry collection): Sinnersphere Productions, 2004.

Dust Radio (poetry collection): Kelp Queen Press, 2007.

Invocabulary (poetry collection): Aqueduct Press, 2018.

New Maps of Hell (poetry collection): self-published, 2019.

JOURNALS AS EDITOR

White Wall Review (with Sarah Wilks) (journal, #16): Ryerson Literary Society, 1991.

ALSO FROM ERIC J. GUIGNARD AND DARK MOON BOOKS:

**EXPLORING DARK SHORT FICTION #3:
A PRIMER TO NISI SHAWL**

Praised by both literary journals and leading fiction magazines, Nisi Shawl is celebrated as an author whose works are lyrical and philosophical, speculative and far-ranging; "…broad in ambition and deep in accomplishment" (*The Seattle Times*). Besides nearly three decades of creating fantasy and science fiction stories, Nisi has also been lauded as editor, journalist, and proponent of feminism, African-American fiction, and other pedagogical issues of diversity.

Dark Moon Books and editor Eric J. Guignard bring you this introduction to her work, the third in a series of primers exploring modern masters of literary dark short fiction. Herein is a chance to discover—or learn more of—the vibrant voice of Nisi Shawl, as beautifully illustrated by artist Michelle Prebich.

Included within these pages are:

- Six short stories, one written exclusively for this book
- Author interview
- Complete bibliography
- Academic commentary by Michael Arnzen, PhD (former humanities chair and professor of the year, Seton Hill University)
- …and more!

Enter this doorway to the vast and fantastic: Get to know Nisi Shawl.

Order your copy at www.darkmoonbooks.com or www.amazon.com
ISBN-13: 978-0-9989383-4-9

ALSO FROM ERIC J. GUIGNARD AND DARK MOON BOOKS:

EXPLORING DARK SHORT FICTION #6: A PRIMER TO RAMSEY CAMPBELL

Hailed by *The Oxford Companion to English Literature* as "Britain's most respected living horror writer," Ramsey Campbell has authored an astounding body of work for over half a century that embodies the weird, the supernatural, and the subtle, much of which is widely considered classics of dark fiction today. He has been given more awards than any other writer in the field, including being made an Honorary Fellow of Liverpool John Moores University for outstanding services to literature.

Dark Moon Books and editor Eric J. Guignard bring you this introduction to his work, the sixth in a series of primers exploring modern masters of literary dark short fiction. Herein is a chance to discover—or learn more of—the remarkable voice of Ramsey Campbell, as beautifully illustrated by artist Michelle Prebich.

Included within these pages are:

- Six short stories, one written exclusively for this book
- Author interview
- Biography and bibliography
- Academic commentary by Michael Arnzen, PhD (former humanities chair and professor of the year, Seton Hill University)
- . . . and more!

Enter this doorway to the vast and fantastic: Get to know Ramsey Campbell.

Order your copy at www.darkmoonbooks.com or www.amazon.com
ISBN-13: 978-1-949491-13-5

ALSO FROM ERIC J. GUIGNARD AND DARK MOON BOOKS:

A WORLD OF HORROR

Every nation of the globe has unique tales to tell, whispers that settle in through the land, creatures or superstitions that enliven the night, but rarely do readers get to experience such a diversity of these voices in one place as in *A WORLD OF HORROR*, the latest anthology book created by award-winning editor Eric J. Guignard, and beautifully illustrated by artist Steve Lines.

Enclosed within its pages are twenty-two all-new dark and speculative fiction stories written by authors from around the world that explore the myths and monsters, fables and fears of their homelands.

Encounter the haunting things that stalk those radioactive forests outside Chernobyl in Ukraine; sample the curious dishes one may eat in Canada; beware the veldt monster that mirrors yourself in Uganda; or simply battle mountain trolls alongside Alfred Nobel in Sweden. These stories and more are found within *A World of Horror*: Enter and discover, truly, there's no place on the planet devoid of frights, thrills, and wondrous imagination.

"This breath of fresh air for horror readers shows the limitless possibilities of the genre."

—*Publishers Weekly* (starred review)

"A fresh collection of horror authors exploring monsters and myths from their homelands."

—*Library Journal*

Order your copy at www.darkmoonbooks.com or www.amazon.com
ISBN-13: 978-0-9989383-1-8

ALSO FROM ERIC J. GUIGNARD AND DARK MOON BOOKS:

POP THE CLUTCH: THRILLING TALES OF ROCKABILLY, MONSTERS, AND HOT ROD HORROR

Welcome to the cool side of the 1950s, where the fast cars and revved-up movie monsters peel out in the night. Where outlaw vixens and jukebox tramps square off with razorblades and lead pipes. Where rockers rock, cool cats strut, and hot rods roar. Where you howl to the moon as the tiki drums pound and the electric guitar shrieks and that spit-and-holler jamboree ain't gonna stop for a long, long time . . . maybe never.

This is the '50s where ghost shows still travel the back roads of the south, and rockabilly has a hold on the nation's youth; where lucky hearts tell the tale, and maybe that fella in the Shriners' fez ain't so square after all. Where exist noir detectives of the supernatural, tattoo artists of another kind, Hollywood fix-it men, and a punk kid with grasshopper arms under his chain-studded jacket and an icy stare on his face.

This is the '50s of *Pop the Clutch: Thrilling Tales of Rockabilly, Monsters, and Hot Rod Horror*. This is your ticket to the dark side of American kitsch . . . the fun and frightful side!

"A fitting tribute to the 1950s with this 18-story compendium of hot rods, rock 'n' roll, and creature features come to life."

—*Publishers Weekly*

Order your copy at www.darkmoonbooks.com or www.amazon.com
ISBN-13: 978-1-949491-01-2

THE CRIME FILES OF KATY GREEN by GENE O'NEILL:

Discover why readers have been applauding this stark, fast-paced noir series by multiple-award-winning author, Gene O'Neill, and follow the dark murder mysteries of Sacramento homicide detectives Katy Green and Johnny Cato, dubbed by the press as Sacramento's "Green Hornet and Cato"!

Book #1: *DOUBLE JACK* (a novella)

400-pound serial killer Jack Malenko has discovered the perfect cover: He dresses as a CalTrans worker and preys on female motorists in distress in full sight of passing traffic. How fast can Katy Green and Johnny Cato track him down before he strikes again?

Book #2: *SHADOW OF THE DARK ANGEL*

Bullied misfit, Samuel Kubiak, is visited by a dark guardian angel who helps Samuel gain just vengeance. There hasn't been a case yet Katy and Johnny haven't solved, but now how can they track a psychopathic suspect that comes and goes in the shadows?

Book #3: *DEATHFLASH*

Billy Williams can see the soul as it departs the body, and is "commanded to do the Lord's work," which he does fanatically, slaying drug addicts in San Francisco . . . Katy and Johnny investigate the case as junkies die all around, for Billy has his own addiction: the rush of viewing the Deathflash.

Order your copy at www.darkmoonbooks.com or www.amazon.com

ALSO FROM GENE O'NEILL AND DARK MOON BOOKS:

A STICK OF DOUBLEMINT

—Book #4 in the series, *THE CRIME FILES OF KATY GREEN*

On a warm San Francisco night, an innocent young woman is gunned down in a gang-related drive-by shooting. The overworked police department have no leads and no suspects, and seemingly little interest in pursuing yet another case involving ongoing gang violence. Then those involved in the shooting start turning up dead, with a stick of Doublemint gum in hand. What does it mean, and who's responsible?

A new detective is assigned to the case, and he quickly realizes he's going to need help to solve it, so turns to old friends, Katy Green and Johnny Cato, now part of a successful private investigation firm!

So begins a race against the clock to stop further murders and to discover the perpetrator. Can the investigating duo, dubbed by newspapers as "Green Hornet and Cato" solve this latest case of the vigilante killings, or will the culprit continue to bloody the city?

Read *A STICK OF DOUBLEMINT* and then continue the shocking case files of Sacramento's "Green Hornet and Cato" with volumes 1–3 (*Double Jack*; *Shadow of the Dark Angel*; and *Deathflash*).

Order your copy at www.darkmoonbooks.com or www.amazon.com
ISBN-13: 978-1-949491-18-0

About Editor, Eric J. Guignard

ERIC J. GUIGNARD IS A writer and editor of dark and speculative fiction, operating from the shadowy outskirts of Los Angeles, where he also runs the small press Dark Moon Books. He's twice won the Bram Stoker Award (the highest literary award of horror fiction), won the Shirley Jackson Award, and been a finalist for the World Fantasy  Award and International Thriller Writers Award.

He has over one hundred stories and non-fiction author credits appearing in publications around the world. As editor, Eric's published multiple fiction anthologies, including his most recent, *Professor Charlatan Bardot's Travel Anthology to the Most (Fictional) Haunted Buildings in the Weird, Wild World* and *A World of Horror*, each a showcase of international horror short fiction.

He currently publishes the acclaimed series of author primers created to champion modern masters of the dark and macabre, *Exploring Dark Short Fiction*. He is also publisher and acquisitions editor for the renowned *+Horror Library+* anthology series. Formerly, he was curator of the series, *The Horror Writers Association Presents: Haunted Library of Horror Classics* through SourceBooks with co-editor Leslie S. Klinger.

His latest books are *Last Case at a Baggage Auction*; *Doorways To The Deadeye*; and short story collection *That Which Grows Wild: 16 Tales of Dark Fiction* (Cemetery Dance). His second collection, *A Graveside Gallery: Tales of Ghosts and Dark Matters*, will be out 2025 (Cemetery Dance) and forthcoming is his next novel, *Wrecked, Yet Sent Forth*.

Outside the glamorous and jet-setting world of indie fiction, Eric's a technical writer and college professor, and he stumbles home each day to a wife, children, dogs, and a terrarium filled with mischievous beetles. Visit Eric at: www.ericjguignard.com, his blog: ericjguignard.blogspot.com, or Twitter: @ericjguignard.

About Academic, Michael Arnzen, PhD

MICHAEL A. ARNZEN (PhD, University of Oregon, 1999) teaches full-time at Seton Hill University, home of the country's only MFA degree in Writing Popular Fiction. To date he has won four Bram Stoker Awards and an International Horror Critics Guild Award for his often funny, always disturbing horror fiction and poetry,  which includes such book-length titles as *Grave Markings*, *Play Dead*, *Freakcidents*, and *Proverbs for Monsters*. Alongside Heidi Ruby Miller, Arnzen also co-edited *Many Genres, One Craft: Lessons in Writing Popular Fiction*—a large how-to guide for authors of speculative fiction and other genres. Arnzen continues to write horror and criticism while teaching the zombie populations near Pittsburgh, PA.

Follow Mike at www.gorelets.com and subscribe to his recently rebooted creative missive, *The Goreletter*.

On top of his genre writing, Arnzen sits on the editorial board for *Paradoxa: Studies in World Literary Genres*, and his academic criticism has appeared in such journals as *Narrative*, *The Journal of Popular Film and Television*, and the *Journal of the Fantastic in the Arts*. He is developing an updated version of his doctoral dissertation, a critical survey of Freud's "unheimlich" in pop culture, called *The Popular Uncanny*.

About Illustrator, Michelle Prebich

MICHELLE PREBICH of Bat in Your Belfry is a Southern California artist whose art and wearable accessories are inspired by history, the natural world, mythology, and Halloween.

She studied Film Production, Theatre, and Fine Art at Cal State Long Beach. She has worn many hats including: production designer, artist, set dresser, property master, and special effects makeup artist.

She often travels and sells original macabre art, art pieces, and apparel she has created through her shop "Bat in Your Belfry" which can be found at www.batinyourbelfry.com and on Instagram @batinyourbelfry.

www.ingramcontent.com/pod-product-compliance
Lightning Source LLC
Chambersburg PA
CBHW032159190726
48289CB00007BA/2300